"A locked-doo very Agatha Christi

"And this one w this day no one k rooms. But people who have stayed here report that all kinds of weird things happen."

"What kinds of things?" Cooper asked.

"Voices," Bryan answered. "Glimpses of shadowy figures. Things disappearing. Faces in the mirrors. Think you can handle it?"

Cooper laughed, and Bryan looked surprised. "I grew up with a ghost," Cooper informed him. "And let's just say that all three of us have friends in the spirit world."

Bryan cocked an eyebrow. "Then this should prove to be very interesting," he said as he inserted the key in the lock and turned it.

Follow the Circle:

circle of three

BOOK
11

the house of
winter

isobel bird

AVON BOOKS

An Imprint of HarperCollinsPublishers

Library of Congress Catalog Card Number: 2001116352

ISBN 0-06-447368-6

First Avon edition, 2001

❖

Visit us on the World Wide Web!
www.harperteen.com

CHAPTER I

"Look at all the snow," Annie said as the car wound its way along the narrow road through the mountains. "I can't believe we're only a couple of hours from Beecher Falls. It's like being in another world."

"It's hard to imagine that there's actually a hotel up here," remarked Cooper. "We haven't seen any houses or anything for a long time."

"The hotel was built in the eighteen hundreds as a place for wealthy people to get away from everything," explained Sophia as she drove her SUV along the snowy road. "It was supposed to feel remote. That's why it's nestled way back in these mountains."

"How did you start using it for retreats?" Annie asked her.

"It's owned by friends of mine," answered Sophia. "Their family built it. Over the years it got harder and harder to maintain the place because people wanted hotels that offered more than just pretty scenery and a remote location. So Fiona and Bryan decided to turn the place into a retreat center.

Now they rent it out to corporations and groups who want to hold gatherings there. Once a year, at the Winter Solstice, they let us use it for the week."

"So they're Wiccan?" Cooper asked.

Sophia shook her head. "Not really," she said. "They're more general all-around pagans. But they're not witches in the usual sense."

"They sound nice," commented Annie.

"They are," Sophia said. "And they have twin daughters who are around your age. Lucy and Nora."

"So, what exactly will we be doing this week?" Cooper inquired.

"A lot of different things," Sophia replied. "You'll find out more about it tonight, but basically this is a week of celebrating Yule and welcoming back the sun after the longest night of the year."

"It's hard to think about the longest night when it's so bright and sunny out right now," Annie joked.

"It will be dark soon enough," said Sophia. "And because there's no town around the hotel to light the place up at night it seems even darker. It's really a wonderful place to celebrate the sabbat."

"Just think," said Annie. "A whole week of rituals and classes and all kinds of stuff. This is the longest we've ever spent doing witchy things."

"I'm really pleased you could all get away for the week," Sophia said. "I think this will be a very special time for all of you, and I hope you get a lot out of it."

"I know I will," Cooper told her. "After the

whole divorce thing with my parents, it will be nice to be with a bunch of witches and not have to worry about all of that."

"And I can certainly use a week away from Aunt Sarah while she gets ready for Becka and Mr. Dunning to come for Christmas," added Annie. "I've never seen her so worked up about anything."

"What about you, Kate?" Sophia asked. "You're awfully quiet back there." She looked at Kate in the rearview mirror and smiled at her. Kate, who was sitting in the backseat with Cooper, gave her a small smile back.

"I think it will be fun," she said simply.

While the others had chatted easily during the ride, Kate had been almost completely silent. The truth was, she *was* excited about the retreat. But she also couldn't help but think about the fact that she was going to see Tyler for the first time since she'd discovered that he and Annie had basically fooled around behind her back. She'd accepted that she and Tyler were probably never going to be a couple again and she'd been able to slowly mend her friendship with Annie, but the wound was still tender. She couldn't deny that.

Sensing Kate's hesitance, Annie and Cooper settled into an uneasy silence. But Sophia, who knew nothing about what had happened among Kate, Tyler, and Annie, continued to talk.

"I love these retreats," she said. "It's nice to just get away from everything and spend time with other witches. It really brings you closer together. A lot of the people who will be here are friends I see only a couple of times a year."

The girls listened as Sophia talked, each of them lost in private thoughts. The fact was, it was a difficult time for each of them. While they were all looking forward to a week in the hotel, they also knew that there were going to be challenges involved with being there. As they drew closer and closer to their destination, they couldn't help but think about what was awaiting them there.

Kate and Cooper, in particular, were relieved to be going on the trip. Mr. and Mrs. Morgan had only reluctantly allowed their daughter to resume attending the weekly Wicca study group, and she'd been sure that they would say no to the trip to the mountains. When asking their permission to go, Kate had tried to make it sound more like a ski trip than a week of ritual and magic. Even so, they had been less than thrilled by her request. To her surprise, however, they'd ultimately agreed that she could go, but only after several long phone calls to Sophia and several anxious days of waiting on Kate's part. Even then, Kate had expected them to retract their permission up until the moment the car had pulled away from their house and she could breathe a sigh of relief.

As for Cooper, her mother was also hesitant about her involvement in the Craft. There had long been an uneasy truce between them regarding the subject, and since Mr. Rivers had moved out of the house, they hadn't spoken about the topic at all. Mrs. Rivers never asked her daughter about class, and Cooper never brought it up. When it came time to mention the trip, Cooper had asked her father's permission first. His reply—"As long as it's okay with your mother"—had both irritated and worried her. She knew that her father was worried about doing anything that might upset the fragile relationship that existed between the three of them because of the separation, but she'd been afraid that perhaps her mother would use the opportunity to make a statement regarding her feelings about witchcraft by denying Cooper permission to go. But when Cooper had mentioned it one morning as her mother was leaving for work she had simply said, "It's up to you. If you want to go, go." While not the enthusiastic support Cooper would have liked, she'd been happy just to have avoided a fight about the matter.

Sophia turned the car onto an even narrower road. It seemed to lead straight into a forest, and the arms of the trees met overhead as they drove through what felt like a tunnel made of shadows and light as the afternoon sun filtered down through the branches of pine. Then they shot out into daylight again, and the girls gasped in unison as they saw what was in front of them.

"Is that it?" Kate asked, her voice filled with awe.

"That's it," confirmed Sophia.

"Wow," Cooper said simply.

"Double wow," echoed Annie.

Before them sat a huge, old hotel. It was situated in the center of a ring of snowy mountains, the tops of which rose up around it. The hotel itself was enormous, an elaborate Victorian building with ornate carvings, several tower rooms with pointed roofs, and stained-glass windows looking out at them like multicolored eyes. Two wings of rooms stretched out on either side of the main building, and smoke puffed gently from several chimneys.

"It's beautiful," Annie said as Sophia pulled the SUV up to the front and parked it beside some other cars that were already there.

"Wait until you see the inside," said Sophia. "Come on."

They got out and retrieved their bags from the back of the car. Then they walked up the neatly shoveled path to the front steps of the hotel and went through the door. Once inside, the girls set down their bags and looked around in awe.

The lobby of the hotel was done in red. Almost everything was red, from the deep red of the walls to the red velvet upholstery on the couches and chairs that were arranged in comfortable groups all around the enormous room. A huge chandelier, its hundreds of individual crystals sparkling with light, hung from the ceiling over their heads, and classical music floated softly through the air.

"Look at that tree," Annie said, nodding at an

enormous pine tree that stood in the center of the lobby. Its spreading branches were strung with what seemed to be thousands of white lights, and ornaments of all kinds hung from it.

"That's the Yule tree," Sophia told them. "The ornaments on it have been used since the hotel opened. Every year they add some new ones, but some of those are almost a hundred and fifty years old."

"Sophia!"

A woman emerged from a doorway behind the long wooden check-in counter, distracting them from looking at the tree. She had deep red hair that complemented the colors of the lobby, and she was wearing a burgundy-colored shirt with jeans. She walked quickly toward them and embraced Sophia warmly.

"Fiona," Sophia said. "Merry meet."

Fiona laughed as she released her friend from the hug. "Merry meet yourself," she replied gaily. "It's been a long time."

"Since last Yule," Sophia said. "How are Bryan and the girls?"

"See for yourself," answered Fiona. Then she turned and called out, "Sophia's here," in a loud voice.

Moments later a man emerged from the doorway. A little shorter than his wife, he had curly black hair and an easy, crooked smile that made his chin dimple. He, too, came over and hugged Sophia.

"Has it really been a whole year?" he asked, shaking his head. "It seems like you were just here."

"It goes by quickly," Sophia told him. "I bet the girls are all grown up now."

"They'll be sixteen this Yule," Bryan said.

"Where are they, honey?" Fiona asked her husband.

"They could be anywhere," he answered. "I'm sure they'll turn up."

"I wanted them to meet *my* girls," Sophia said. "Bryan and Fiona, this is Cooper, Kate, and Annie. They're part of my group this year."

Fiona and Bryan shook hands with the three girls. "You willingly signed up for her boot camp?" Bryan asked them, cocking his head at Sophia. "You're braver than I am."

"She's not so bad once you get the drill down," Cooper deadpanned.

Bryan laughed as Sophia pretended to be horrified by Cooper's remark. Then the front door opened and another group of people came in.

"Bryan, why don't you take this bunch up to their rooms while I say hello to the new arrivals," Fiona said.

"Will do," answered Bryan. "Follow me, folks," he added to Kate, Annie, Cooper, and Sophia.

They picked up their bags and followed as Bryan walked down the hallway that stretched to the left away from the lobby. The corridor seemed to go on forever, then they came to a staircase and Bryan started up it.

"We saved you the best rooms in the house," he remarked as they climbed.

"Ah," Sophia said. "The ghost rooms."

"That would be them," Bryan replied.

"Ghost rooms?" Annie asked.

"Indeed," Bryan told her. "Didn't Sophia tell you that the hotel is haunted?"

"By who?" Cooper said.

"All kinds of people," said Bryan as they ascended another flight of stairs. "Doomed lovers. Murdered gangsters. Failed businessmen. All kinds of people died in this place."

"How cheery," remarked Kate grimly as she switched her bag to her other shoulder. "So, which ones do we get?"

Bryan went up a final set of stairs, and they found themselves in another hallway. "You get the best ones of all," he told them as they walked halfway down and stopped in front of a door. Bryan took out a key and held it up. "You get the honeymoon ghosts."

The girls looked at each other. "Okay," Cooper said, "I'll bite. What's the story?"

Bryan grinned wickedly. "It's quite a story," he replied. "It happened in 1923. A young couple, Rose and Edgar Whiting, came to the hotel to get married and to spend their honeymoon here. It was a grand affair. They rented the entire place. The rooms were filled with their guests. On the day they married, Rose was beautiful in her wedding dress and Edgar was as handsome as could be in his tuxedo. The wedding party afterward was legendary, lasting long into the night. Finally, in the early hours of the morning, the couple retired to these rooms."

Bryan paused dramatically, letting them all wonder what could possibly come next. After an agonizing wait, he continued. "When the maid came in the morning to bring Rose and Edgar their breakfasts, she found them . . . dead."

"Dead how?" Annie asked.

"Aren't you a morbid one?" commented Bryan, looking at Annie curiously.

"It's not a good story unless we know the how part," Cooper explained.

"This is quite a bunch you have here," Bryan said to Sophia. Then he turned back to the girls. "That's the strange part," he said. "Rose had been poisoned and Edgar had been shot through the heart. But no one could tell which of them had died first, so they never knew if it was murder or some kind of suicide pact."

"Why would they kill themselves on their wedding night?" Kate said. "That doesn't make sense. Of course, they had to have been murdered."

"That's what the police thought," Bryan said. "Except that the door was locked from the inside. The maid had to use her key to open it."

"But if she had a key, someone else could have

had one as well, right?" said Cooper skeptically.

"There were only two of them," Bryan said. "This is one of them." He waved the key in his hand at them. "The other one is in the hotel office."

"A locked-door mystery," Annie said. "How very Agatha Christie."

"And this one was never solved," Bryan said. "To this day no one knows what happened in these rooms. But people who have stayed here report that all kinds of weird things happen."

"What kinds of things?" Cooper asked.

"Voices," Bryan answered. "Glimpses of shadowy figures. Things disappearing. Faces in the mirrors. Think you can handle it?"

Cooper laughed, and Bryan looked surprised. "I grew up with a ghost," Cooper informed him. "And let's just say that all three of us have friends in the spirit world."

Bryan cocked an eyebrow. "Then this should prove to be very interesting," he said as he inserted the key in the lock and turned it.

The door swung open silently as Bryan motioned for them to enter. Kate stepped inside first and gave a little scream. The others rushed forward to see what had startled her, and were surprised to see a girl standing in the room. She looked back at them blankly, as if they had interrupted her doing something.

"Nora," Bryan said. "What are you doing in here?"

The girl pushed her long red hair back from her face and looked around the room. "Oh," she said. "I just came in to make sure everything was clean. Mom told me you were going to put people in here this week."

The girl smiled at Kate and the others. "It's not every day that someone stays in the ghost rooms," she told them.

"Everyone, this is my daughter Nora," Bryan said.

The girls all nodded and said hello, and Nora smiled back at them. "Hi," she said.

"Where's Lucy?" Bryan asked his daughter.

Nora shrugged. "I don't know," she said. "Last time I saw her, she was going to see if they needed any help in the kitchen."

"I'm right here," said a voice from the doorway.

They all turned and saw another girl standing there. She was an exact copy of her sister, right down to the clothes she was wearing. She stepped inside the room and greeted the girls and Sophia. Then she looked at Nora. "I was looking for you," she said, her voice even but not warm.

"Sorry," Nora said. "I was right here."

"Well," Bryan said. "We should get you girls settled. Annie and Cooper, I thought we'd put the two of you in this room. And Kate," he added, walking to a door set into one wall of the room, "I thought you could sleep in the adjoining room with your friend Sasha when she arrives."

"Sounds good to me," said Kate, peering through the door into the other bedroom. "So, where did the honeymooners die?"

"In this room," Nora said quickly.

The others looked at her, and she blushed. "Sorry," she said. "I didn't mean to sound like some kind of death freak or something. It's just that when you live here you kind of get used to telling the story."

"Tell me about it," Cooper remarked. "I get to tell the story of the ghost in my house about ten times a week during the summer."

"You live with a ghost?" Nora asked, sounding interested.

Cooper nodded. "I'll tell you all about it later."

"I'd like that," said Nora.

"But right now you and I have some chores to do," Lucy said.

Nora's face fell, but she nodded. "Lucy's right," she said. "We'll see you guys later."

The girls left. Then Bryan said, "Sophia, I'll show you to your room now. It's down the hall. Girls, if you need anything just call the front desk. Otherwise we'll see you at dinner tonight. It's at six in the dining room downstairs. Oh, and here's the room key. Don't lose it, now. There's just the one."

Annie took the key from him and put it in her pocket. Bryan and Sophia left, shutting the door behind them.

"Can you believe this place?" Cooper asked,

looking around the room. It was furnished with antiques, including two huge wooden beds that faced a fireplace. The windows opened out on to a balcony, and the view was incredible.

"Wait until you see the bathroom," Kate called from that very room. "We have a huge claw-foot bathtub."

"Ghosts or no ghosts, this is going to be a fantastic week," said Annie.

"What about those twins?" Cooper said. "Nora seems nice, but what was Lucy's problem?"

"She seemed a little uptight," agreed Annie.

"Maybe she's just weirded out by the idea of all these witches being here," suggested Kate, emerging from the bathroom.

"Maybe," Annie said. "But there was definitely tension between them."

"Not our problem," Cooper replied, stretching out on one of the beds. "I don't know about you guys, but for the next five days I am *not* going to get caught up in any drama. Life has been exciting enough recently."

Kate and Annie glanced at each other and then looked away.

"Right," Kate said. "This week should be about having fun."

"Yeah," Annie said unconvincingly. "Fun."

CHAPTER 2

A little before six o'clock the girls went downstairs to the lobby. They had each bathed and changed, and they were anxious to see who had arrived since they had. There had been no sign of Sasha, and they were wondering where she was. They found out when they entered the lobby and saw her standing at the reception desk with Thea.

"Hey, girlfriends!" Sasha exclaimed when she saw Annie, Kate, and Cooper. She ran over and gave them all big hugs. "Isn't this place the coolest?"

"What took you guys so long?" Cooper asked.

"Oh, you know Mom," Sasha said, rolling her eyes. "Do I bring the white robe or the blue robe? The pink crystal or the black crystal? The mint tea or the dandelion tea?"

They all laughed. It was good to see Sasha talking about Thea as if they'd lived together forever. Really, Thea had only been appointed Sasha's legal guardian earlier in the year, after Sasha's parents had given up custody of her.

"Honey, I've got my room key," Thea said, coming up to greet the girls. "But they say you're in another room."

"Right," Annie said. "You're with us."

"Goddess help us," commented Thea kindly. "Well, I'm going up to change before dinner. Do you want to come?"

"I'm fine," Sasha told her. "I'll take my stuff up later."

"Okay, then," Thea told her. "I'll see you all in a while."

"Can you believe this place?" Sasha said as the four of them sat on one of the big couches in the lobby. "It's like something out of *The Shining*."

"You and your Stephen King fetish," Cooper teased. "But this time you're not far off. The place *is* haunted."

"Or at least that's what they told us," said Annie.

"I believe it," Sasha replied. "This place just screams haunted."

"Wait until she hears what happened in our room," said Annie.

"What?" Sasha said excitedly. "Tell."

Kate started to tell her the story of Rose and Edgar Whiting. But she got only as far as the part about it being their wedding night when she stopped.

"What's wrong?" Sasha asked. "You're all pale. Don't tell me you're seeing ghosts already?"

Kate shook her head. "Not quite," she answered.

The others turned and followed her gaze to where Tyler was standing in the doorway of the hotel. He was with his mother and his sister. They were bringing their bags in, and Tyler hadn't seen them yet. But a moment later he did. For a brief moment, a strange look came over his face. Then he smiled and waved. They all waved back.

"Stop staring," Sasha ordered, not looking directly at either Kate or Annie. "Tell me the rest of the story."

"Oh, right," said Kate, sounding distracted. "Where were we?"

"At the beginning," Sasha said.

Kate began the story again. She was almost at the part where the door was locked from the inside when Tyler walked over to them. "Hey," he said.

Sasha groaned. "You have got the *worst* timing," she told him.

Tyler's face fell. "What did I do?" he asked, confused.

"Nothing," Cooper reassured him. "Kate was just telling Sasha about the couple who died in our room."

Tyler nodded, then looked at Cooper sharply. "Died?" he said.

"We're not starting over again," Sasha told him. "Here's the Cliffs Notes version: couple gets married, maid finds them dead the next morning, no one knows who killed whom. Now you're up to speed. Keep going, Kate."

"There's not much more to tell," Kate told her. "The room was locked from the inside, and people claim that weird stuff happens in there. That's about it."

Sasha clapped her hands together. "I love it," she said happily. "Tragedy and murder and ghosts, all in one place. This is my kind of hotel."

"Wow," Tyler said. "And to think that all I was worried about was getting a room with a view. I didn't know there was a ghost option."

"Tyler," said his sister, coming up to them, "here's your room key." She handed him a key and then smiled at the girls. "Hi, guys," she said.

"Hi, Hannah," Kate answered while the others waved.

"It's almost dinnertime," Hannah told Tyler. "We're going to go up."

"I'll come, too," Tyler told her. "I guess I'll see you all at dinner," he added to the others.

When Tyler and Hannah were gone there was a strained silence for a minute. Then Sasha broke the tension by saying, "I know it's Yule and all, but if I see one piece of fruitcake this week there's no telling what I'll do."

"Where did that come from?" Cooper asked her, laughing.

"I was just thinking about Christmas and all of that," said Sasha. "I hate fruitcake."

"And it's always said such nice things about you," Annie remarked.

They all giggled at the silliness of the conversation. Then Kate said, "I think it's time we found this dining room."

They got up and walked through the lobby. Several other people seemed to be wandering in a particular direction, so they followed them. A minute later they found themselves walking into an enormous dining room. There were numerous round tables scattered throughout the room, each one decorated with a white cloth and white roses in beautiful arrangements.

"They really know how to do this right," commented Sasha as the girls walked around the room. They selected a table and sat down. In addition to the four of them, there were four empty chairs at the table. The other tables in the room were filling up quickly as more and more people came in, and the girls were happy to see their friend Archer enter, look around, and make a beeline for their table.

"Mind if I join you?" she asked, then sat when they all nodded their heads and Cooper pointed to a chair.

"Who are all these people?" Annie asked her.

Archer looked around. "Well, a lot of them you know from class and from the covens in town," she said. "The rest come from all over. This is sort of like the Midsummer gathering, only much more serious."

Cooper, Kate, and Annie shared a look after

hearing Archer's comment. The Midsummer gathering, which had taken place in the woods outside of Beecher Falls, had been more than a little unsettling to each of them, for very different reasons.

"What do you mean, more serious?" Annie inquired carefully.

Archer took a breath. "It's just that Yule is a more solemn time of year," she said. "Midsummer is all about partying and playing. Yule is about calling the light back on the longest night. It's a time of reflection and looking to the future. Midsummer is all about fun."

"Some fun," Cooper said under her breath, remembering her particularly unpleasant experiences on that night.

"Not that Yule isn't fun," Archer continued. "It's a lot of fun. But there's something darker about it. I guess it's because long ago, when people's lives really were ruled by the seasons and by the weather, this time of year seemed pretty bleak. They'd had nothing but snow and ice and blackness for several months. It probably seemed like spring would never arrive."

"What about Christmas?" said Sasha. "Presents and all of that are kind of fun."

"Don't even get me started on Christmas," Archer said. "It has almost nothing to do with Yule. But we'll get into all of that during the week. Well, depending on which path you choose to do."

"Path?" Kate asked.

"You'll find out all about that in a little bit," Archer said mysteriously.

The girls tried to get her to tell them more, but she wouldn't. She just kept saying that they would have to wait and find out. Luckily, they were distracted when three other people joined their table. One was Ben, another student from their weekly Wicca study class, and the other two were older women they had never met before but whom Archer seemed to know well.

"Everybody, this is Star and Ivy," Archer said, introducing the women. "They run a coven called the Daughters of Diana."

"It's actually more like a cooperative farm turned coven," Ivy said, her bright blue eyes twinkling mischievously in her lined and sun-browned face. "We started off raising goats and organic vegetables almost thirty years ago. The coven part came later. That was her fault," she added, nodding at Star.

"Oh, blame it all on me," said the other woman, whose gray hair was tied in a thick braid and who wore a T-shirt with a Greenpeace logo on it. "You were the one who brought home the book on witchcraft."

"But *you* were the one who suggested we do that first ritual," Ivy teased.

"It's no use arguing with her," Star said to the girls. "She always has to win. But it doesn't matter. However it got started, our coven has been going for a long time. This is our fifteenth Yule retreat here at the hotel. I think we've been coming ever since the first one."

"Do you still raise goats on the farm?" Annie asked.

"Oh, yes," Ivy answered. "But only for the milk. We make cheese out of it. And we have bees now, too."

"You girls should come visit us this summer," Star suggested. "We do weeklong events there that you might enjoy." Then she turned to Ben. "I'd invite you, too, but we're a women-only coven," she informed him, smiling. "Not that we wouldn't welcome a visit when we aren't holding an event. How do you feel about shoveling goat manure?"

"I think maybe I'd be better with the bees," joked Ben.

Ivy and Star told them more about their farm and about their coven while they waited for dinner to start. The room rustled with conversations as the tables filled up and old friends found one another and began chatting. But all the talking ceased when a bell sounded from the front of the room and everyone looked up to see what was happening.

Standing at the head of the room was a man. He was short and heavy and balding, and he seemed very cheery. "He looks like the mayor of Munchkinland," Cooper whispered to Kate, forcing Kate to stifle a laugh by putting her hand over her mouth.

"Greetings," the man said, his voice clear and

warm. "As many of you know, I am Bilbo." Scattered laughter ran through the room as people acknowledged the man's reference to the short, round hero of the classic fantasy novel *The Hobbit*, whom he very much resembled.

"We are here in this beautiful hotel to celebrate another Yule," Bilbo said. "And once again our thanks go out to Fiona and Bryan Reilly for their wonderful hospitality."

Applause erupted at the mention of the Reillys, and the two of them stood up from the table at which they were sitting and waved.

"And of course we also thank the wonderful staff," Bilbo continued. "And particularly everyone's favorite head chef, Laurel Stewart."

The applause for the chef was even louder than that for the Reillys, as people whistled and clapped and called out Laurel's name. A moment later a smiling woman with black hair and dark eyes poked her head into the room and waved a wooden spoon at everyone.

"I have soup waiting for me back there in the kitchen," she said. "Otherwise I'd stick around."

When Laurel had disappeared again, Bilbo continued his introduction. "As I said, we're all here to celebrate Yule. But we're here to work, too. As we do every year, we've come up with four different paths for you to choose from. Whichever one you choose, you will work with that path for the remainder of the week. Each path has a different focus, and so now I will turn the festivities over to the four leaders of those paths. Each one will tell you what her or his path is all about this year. Then you can decide which one is right for you. So let's get to it. We don't want any charges of favoritism here, so we're just going to go in circle-casting order and start with the Air path."

Bilbo stepped aside and a woman took his place. She was slender, with skin the color of copper and black hair that hung loosely over her shoulders. "Merry meet," she said. "I am Maia, and I will be leading the Air path this year. Our path will focus on using the creative talents of words and music to give birth to the ideas that have been germinating inside of us during the winter."

A second woman stood up and said in a loud voice, "I'm Luna, and I'm leading the Fire path. Fire is an integral part of Yule, as it symbolizes the return of warmth and light, and our focus in the Fire path will be on rekindling the fire within ourselves. If there are any of you out there who feel like you need a little jump start going into the new season, this path is for you. Oh, and don't join us if you're afraid of dancing, because we plan on doing a lot of it." She raised her arms and shook her body, making everyone cheer.

After Luna, a man walked to the front. He was tall and thin, with dark blond hair and little round glasses. "I'm Jackson," he said quietly. "I'm the leader for Water path, and what I'm going to focus on during the week is exploring the deep water within us that we're afraid to dive into. Yule is a time of darkness pierced by light, and we're going to use meditation and ritual to go into our own darkness and see what we find there." He paused a moment and then added, smiling, "It's not really as gloomy as it sounds. We're going to have fun, too."

People laughed as Jackson returned to his seat, but the laughter died out as the fourth leader came forward. She was quite old, and seemed rather frail. When she spoke her voice was soft. "My name is Ginny," she said. "You'll have to excuse me. This is the first time I've ever done anything like this. But I'm doing it, and I'll be leading the Earth path."

Ginny started to walk back to her seat when several people called out, "And what's it about?"

Ginny stopped. "I told you I've never done this before," she joked. "Earth path this year is going to be about death. Not just death, but death and rebirth and how we think about those things. It's not going to be an easy path, but I think it will be very rewarding."

Ginny sat down and Bilbo once again took center stage. "There you have it, folks," he said. "We hope one of those paths appeals to you, because they're all we've got. But you don't have to decide right now which one you want to walk. Enjoy your dinners. When you're done, the four leaders will be sitting at their tables waiting for you. Find the person whose path you're interested in and introduce yourself. Right now, though, I think I smell some amazing food waiting to be eaten, so come and get it."

Dinner was served as a buffet, and the girls lined up with the others to see what awaited them. When they got to the table they discovered all kinds of wonderful things, from several different salads to vegetarian lasagna, pasta with Thai peanut sauce, and baked eggplant. Each dish smelled better than the one before it, and when they went back to their table their plates were piled high.

"So, which paths are you all thinking about?" Ivy asked them after they'd eaten a little bit and weren't so hungry.

"I think I'm leaning toward Fire," Ben answered, his mouth full of eggplant. "It's been a long winter, and I could use a little boost."

"That one sounded good to me, too," Sasha said. "Especially the dancing part."

"Luna is a wonderful teacher," Star told them. "I've taken her paths before, and they're always great. But I think this year I'm going for Water. There's something about it that I like."

"Yes," Ivy said. "You like the fact that it sounds dark. You always did like the crone aspect of the Goddess best."

"Maybe because I'm practically one myself," joked Star. She added to the others, "I'll be sixty-seven in June."

"I'm thinking about Water as well," Kate said

suddenly. The others looked at her. "It just sounds interesting," she said, without elaborating before turning her attention back to her pasta salad.

"Not to me," said Cooper. "I'm Air all the way. Words and music? What could be more perfect?"

"Cooper writes songs and performance pieces," Annie explained to Star and Ivy, who nodded.

"What about you, Annie?" asked Archer. "Do you have a path in mind?"

Annie sighed. "There's one I like," she said. "But I'm kind of afraid of it, so I don't know for sure yet."

"Sometimes being afraid of something means it's exactly where you need to go," Ivy remarked.

They continued to eat, going back for seconds and even thirds of their favorite dishes. When everyone had eaten enough, they looked around to see which paths people were choosing. The four leaders were sitting at different tables, and the people interested in their paths were gathered around them.

"It looks like I'll have a lot of company in Air," Cooper said as she surveyed the large crowd surrounding Maia.

Ben and Sasha headed for the Fire table, leaving Kate and Annie looking from one table to the next, trying to make their final decisions.

"I'm off to jump into Water," Star said to Kate. "Care to join me?"

"Sure," Kate said, and the two of them left.

"Looks like we're the two holdouts," commented Ivy to Annie. "Archer is over there with the Airheads."

Annie laughed at the joke. "Do you know where you're going?" she asked Ivy.

"I know where I *want* to go," Ivy said. "But I'm like you—I'm not sure if I can really do it."

"I will if you will," Annie told her.

"It's a deal," said Ivy. "So, where are you going?"

Annie took a deep breath. "Death," she said.

Ivy laughed. "Well, let's go then," she told Annie. "Because that's exactly where I'm headed, too."

She held out her hand and Annie took it. "Here goes nothing," Annie said as the two of them walked toward Ginny's table.

CHAPTER 3

"The fear of water is one of the most primal fears that humans have."

Kate sat, cross-legged, in a circle with the other members of the Water path. It was Sunday morning. They'd just finished a delicious breakfast, and now they were gathered in the hotel library. The leader of each path had selected a different room to hold meetings in, and Kate was pleased by Jackson's choice. The library was huge, with shelves that ran from the floor to the ceiling and were filled with all kinds of books. Enormous windows at one end let in tons of light, and Kate felt warm and happy, if a little bit apprehensive. She still didn't know quite what was going to happen. But at least Star was in her group, as were a few other people she knew from having attended various rituals over the year. Most important, Tyler *wasn't* in the Water path. He had chosen Fire, so he was Sasha's problem for the week. That at least made Kate feel somewhat more relaxed.

"But why do so many of us fear the water?" asked Jackson.

"Because it hides things," said a woman to Kate's left. "You can't usually see what's under it, and it could be anything."

"Like what?" Jackson prodded.

"I don't know," the woman answered. "Rocks, maybe."

"Sharks," a man across the circle said, prompting nervous laughter.

"Sunken boats," added someone else. "I have a recurring dream where I'm in the water and a huge boat is sinking in front of me. It's absolutely terrifying, not because I'm afraid of drowning or anything but because the idea of something so big being swallowed up by the water and dragged underneath me is just horrible."

Jackson nodded as each person spoke. "These are all excellent answers," he said. "We're afraid of water because it conceals things that might be frightening or dangerous, and also because if we get in too deep we might not be able to get out and we could drown. But water can also be life-saving, right? We need it to live. And if we allow ourselves to float on it, water will hold us up indefinitely. But most of us would rather fight against the water than let it do that. Why?"

"It's just a natural instinct," said Kate. "It's like learning to swim. When you first jump into the water you splash and kick because you're afraid if you don't you'll sink. It takes a while to figure out that you have to work with the water instead of against it."

"Exactly," said Jackson. "And that's what this path is about. We're going to talk about how we work *with* the water in our lives instead of struggling against it. Let me ask you all this, what does water represent in witchcraft?"

"Mystery," said several people at once.

"Secrets," said another.

"The unknown," a third suggested.

"Good," Jackson said. "So if it represents those things, then what we're talking about is figuring out how to work with mystery and the unknown without being overly afraid of it. We're talking about allowing ourselves to experience the wonder and the power of going into darkness, even when we don't know what's waiting there for us."

Kate felt a little shiver of fear run down her spine as she suddenly imagined herself walking down a dark corridor, unable to see what was ahead of her or to either side. The image both frightened and excited her.

"But can't that be dangerous?"

Kate looked over at Lucy Reilly, the person who had just asked the question. She'd been sort of surprised to see that Lucy was in her group, or that she was in any group. She'd assumed that the Reilly girls would be working during the week, not taking part in the activities. But there Lucy was, holding a notebook and pen in her hands and looking at Jackson with a mixture of expectation and sullenness, as if daring him to contradict her. Kate hadn't even spoken to Lucy, but already she'd decided that the girl had a bad attitude about things. She seemed determined to be unhappy, and Kate didn't like that. Nora seemed much more easygoing, and Kate found herself wishing that the other twin was in her group instead of Lucy.

"Yes," Jackson said. "It can be dangerous. But anything can be dangerous, especially magic. It's what you do with it that's important."

Lucy nodded and didn't say anything. Kate found herself staring at the girl. She didn't know why. She couldn't help it. There was just something about her face, about how intent she looked as she wrote in her notebook. It was as if Lucy was desperately trying to figure out something but wasn't quite there. Her forehead was knitted up and her eyes were focused on the page in front of her as she wrote.

Then, suddenly, she looked up and straight into Kate's face. Kate tried to look away, but it was too late. Lucy had seen her. Kate glanced back and saw Lucy watching her with an irritated expression. *Great*, she thought. *Now she'll* really *like me*. She tried to smile at Lucy, but the other girl turned back to her notes and totally ignored her.

"As the week goes on we'll go deeper and deeper into the water—into mystery," Jackson was saying. "We're going to confront those things that may be holding us back and preventing us from doing the things we want to do in our magical work."

"What exactly will we be doing?" asked Star.

Jackson gave her a sly smile. "That's part of the mystery," he said. "I'm only going to let you see one step ahead at a time. I don't want you to see any more than that because the point of this path is to learn to trust yourself, as well as the others you're working with, to walk into the unknown and face whatever is there."

Star leaned over to Kate. "It looks like we really asked for it this time," she said. "You still want to do it?"

"Yeah," Kate said. "I think I do."

As much as what Jackson had been saying frightened her, Kate was intrigued by the prospect of seeing where the path might take her. She'd always been a little bit afraid of going where she couldn't see, in life and especially in her magic. Cooper and Annie took chances, but she almost always played it safe. Her recent experiences with the practices of Santeria, which she had studied for a month as part of the study group, had been a big step for her. Thanks to what she'd learned from Evelyn LeJardin, the woman who had taught her what she now knew about the religion, Kate had discovered a part of herself that she hadn't known existed.

In particular, being told that she was under the protection of the Santerian god Oggun had given her the courage to experiment with magic. Her experiment hadn't been entirely successful, but she'd learned from it, and that was the important thing. Now she thought she was ready to take another step forward, to see what else lay along the path she'd chosen to walk.

"Okay," Jackson said. "Why don't we start with our first exercise. I'd like you all to put on one of these."

He opened a box that had been sitting beside him and handed it to the person on his right. She removed a long strip of black cloth and held it up before passing the box to the next person.

"These are blindfolds," Jackson explained. "There's one for each of you. When you get yours, tie it around your eyes. And make sure you can't see out the bottom or the sides," he added sternly. "I don't want any cheating."

As each person took a blindfold she or he put it on. Kate took hers and placed it over her eyes. She was surprised at how the light was cut off instantly and she was plunged into darkness. As she knotted the ends of the blindfold behind her head, she was reminded of the night when she, Annie, and Cooper had undergone their dedication ceremony beginning their year and a day of studying Wicca. They had been blindfolded then, too, and she had been extremely nervous. She hadn't known what the witches were going to do to her, or what was expected of her.

She felt a little bit like that now, but this time she knew that nothing bad was going to happen to her. She knew that she was among friends, even if she didn't know most of the people in her path. She also knew that Jackson wouldn't let anything bad occur, and that made things easier.

"All right," Jackson said. "It looks as if you all have blindfolds on. Now I'd like you all to stand up."

Kate felt around and carefully pushed herself up off the floor. Standing was more difficult than she'd expected without anything to hang on to or any way of knowing where she was. But she did it, and all around her she heard the others standing as well.

"Now I want you to make sure you're still in a circle," Jackson said. "Everyone take the hands of the people on either side of you."

Kate reached out, feeling for hands. She found one and closed her fingers around the other person's. It felt good to have something to hold. With her other hand she waved around until she met someone else doing the same thing. The two of them laughed, and Kate could tell that the other person was a man by the sound of his voice. She gripped his hand and he moved to stand closer to her.

Jackson was walking around them, and Kate could hear his voice getting closer and farther away as he moved. "That's good," he said. "There are still a few of you who only have one hand being held.

Keep looking until you've found another."

A minute later he said, "Perfect. You've accomplished your first task. But don't get excited. It gets harder now."

There were groans from the participants at that news. Kate wondered what Jackson would make them do next, and if she could do it. She felt secure standing in a circle with people on either side of her, and she didn't want that to change. But she suspected that Jackson had other ideas for them.

"Now I want you to drop the hands of the people beside you," he said.

Kate let go and felt the fingers slipping out of hers. As soon as her neighbors had let go she felt alone. She stood there, her body swaying slightly. She wished that someone would reach out and touch her. Suddenly she was overcome by the irrational thought that everyone except her had left the room, and that she was standing there all alone. Or worse, that everyone else had somehow been instructed to take off their blindfolds and they were all standing there, watching her. She almost reached up to remove her own blindfold when Jackson began to speak again.

"I want you all to turn around," he said. "Just keep turning until you hear me say stop."

Kate began to turn slowly, moving her feet carefully so that she wouldn't fall down. Why was Jackson having them do this? she wondered. What purpose could it possibly have? All it seemed to be doing was making her dizzy and disoriented. But she continued to turn until she was totally unsure of whether she was facing forward or backward or somewhere in between.

"Okay," Jackson called out. "Stop."

Kate froze. Her head was still reeling a little, but that passed after a moment. She still didn't know which way she was facing, however.

"Now I want you all to walk forward," instructed Jackson. "Go as slowly as you need to, but walk straight ahead. And when you find yourself bumping into someone, stop and take that person's hand."

Kate hesitated. She was having a hard time willing her feet to go forward. What if she tripped over something? What if there was no one in front of her and she just kept walking until she hit a wall?

"Don't worry about falling," said Jackson. "I'll be walking around watching you. And if you're really going nowhere I'll give you a little nudge in the right direction."

Hearing that made Kate feel slightly better, and she stepped forward. She was still worried about tripping, and about running into someone else, but she did it. She put her hands out in front of her so that she could feel anything she came into contact with.

She took half a dozen steps without touching anything. All around the room she could hear people moving, but she wasn't running into any of them. Was she going the right way? What *was* the right way? She had no way of knowing.

Every so often she heard people cry out in triumph as they found someone else in their path. She'd been moving around for a long time. Was she the only one who hadn't yet partnered up? She began to panic again, but then she remembered that Jackson was watching to make sure nothing bad happened. Still, she was anxious to find someone.

Then her hands touched something. It felt soft. It disappeared for a second, and Kate found herself trying to find it again. Then it was there, under her fingers. It was a shirtsleeve. She ran her hands down the person's arm until she found a hand, which she gripped in triumph.

"I thought I was going to end up all by myself," Kate said.

"So did I," said a female voice.

"It looks as if everyone has found a partner," Jackson said. "But don't take off your blindfolds yet. Now I want you to sit down facing your partner."

Kate and her partner held hands as they lowered themselves to the floor and positioned themselves so that they were directly in front of one another. They continued to hold hands, as if neither of them wanted to let go again now that they'd found someone to touch.

"Okay," Jackson said. "Now for the really fun part. Each of you is going to tell your partner a secret about yourself. And that secret is going to be what it is you are most afraid of."

Kate felt her heart stop in her chest as Jackson

spoke. She had to tell this person she couldn't even see what it was she was most afraid of in the world? She couldn't do that.

"I don't want you to say things like snakes or heights or really big dogs," Jackson continued. "Really think about it. Think about what it is you most fear in this world. Once you know, tell your partner."

Kate was still holding her partner's hand, and she felt her fingers stiffen. *Is she as afraid as I am?* Kate wondered. *No, make that terrified.* She was being asked to tell a complete stranger her biggest fear. How could she do that?

But she's blindfolded, too, she reminded herself. *You can't see each other.* Strangely, that made things worse instead of better. It meant that she couldn't see the other person's face. She couldn't tell whether her partner was someone she knew or a stranger. She was just a pair of hands and a voice.

"Wow," Kate said finally. "This is hard."

"Don't talk too much," Jackson warned them, making Kate jump. "Work quickly. You're trying to make it easier, and this isn't supposed to be easy."

Kate breathed deeply. Should she go first? Should she wait for her partner? The other person wasn't saying anything either. Were they both just going to sit there forever? Finally, Kate couldn't stand it any longer.

"I'm afraid of never trusting anyone again," she said, surprising herself. She hadn't been thinking that at all. She'd been thinking about how she was afraid that she wouldn't be able to make a decision when the time came to choose whether or not to be initiated into Wicca as a full-fledged witch. But at the last second the other statement had come out.

Now that it had, she realized that it was true. She was afraid of never trusting anyone. The situation with Tyler and Annie had weakened the trust she'd had with each of them, and now she saw that it had shaken her more than she'd been letting herself believe.

But it wasn't the time to think about that. She was supposed to be listening to her partner. She tried to focus on the person whose hands she was holding. But she wasn't saying anything. Kate could hear her breathing, and could feel her fingers trembling, but she wasn't speaking. Then her voice came, quickly and trembling.

"I'm afraid my sister is going to kill me," she said.

The words hit Kate like a splash of cold water. But before she could react to them Jackson said, "It's time to stand up again. When you're on your feet I want you to spin around again. When I say stop, stop and walk forward twelve paces. Then you may take off your blindfolds."

Wait! Kate cried out silently. *I can't just leave things this way.* Her partner had just told her that she feared for her life. If Kate did as Jackson asked, she wouldn't know who she'd been talking to.

But her partner was standing, pulling Kate with her. Reluctantly, Kate got up as well. She wanted to pull her blindfold off, but she didn't dare. Then her partner let go of her hands, and Kate was alone again.

"Spin," Jackson said. "Spin until I say stop."

Kate did as he said, turning around and around. As she did the words her partner had spoken kept repeating in her mind. *I'm afraid my sister is going to kill me. I'm afraid my sister is going to kill me. I'm afraid my sister is going to kill me.*

"Stop," Jackson called out. "Now walk forward and take off your blindfolds."

Kate moved ahead, no longer caring whether she fell or ran into someone else. She counted out twelve steps, then reached up and removed her blindfold. Blinking in the sudden harshness of the light, she looked around. Who had her partner been? Where was she now? People were all over the library, each of them staring around. There were several women around Kate. Her partner could have been any of them. She had no way of knowing for sure which of them it had been.

"Wasn't that intense?"

Kate looked up and saw Star standing a few feet from her. Had she been her partner? Kate tried to remember how the voice had sounded, but suddenly it was slipping away from her. She looked at Star and smiled weakly.

"Yeah," she said. "That's one word for it."

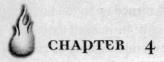

CHAPTER 4

"I didn't realize when we picked Air that they were going to take it so literally," said Cooper, rubbing her hands together. She was standing on the top of a small hill that sat behind the hotel. Maia had led them on a short hike to get to it, and now the group was arranged in a circle. The winter sun was bright overhead, but it was still cold. Cooper was glad she'd remembered to bring her ski jacket with her on the trip. Otherwise she would have been freezing.

"At least it's not snowing," said the person she was speaking to. Cooper was standing next to Nora, and like her, the other girl was rubbing her hands together as they waited to see what Maia had in store for them. "Maybe we should have picked the Fire path," Nora joked. "I bet they're sitting in the lobby toasting marshmallows and drinking cocoa."

Cooper laughed. She liked Nora's sense of humor. She was sort of sarcastic, much like Cooper was, and while she seemed into what they were doing she didn't treat it like something that they had to take too seriously. Cooper was glad to have someone else her own age in the Air path.

"Feel the air," Maia called out to them. She was standing in the center of the circle with her arms held out and her face turned up to the sky. Her long hair was blowing gently in the steady breeze that swept over the hilltop, and the snow that was on the ground swirled around her as if something invisible were running its fingertips across the ground.

"Maybe they should have called this the pneumonia path," Nora whispered to Cooper as they imitated Maia and stood embracing the wind.

"Breathe the air in," Maia told them. "Let it fill you."

"I feel like a balloon," said Cooper to Nora. "If I suck in any more air I'm going to float away over those mountains."

The two of them giggled, earning stern looks from some of the older people around them, all of whom seemed to be intently attempting to become one with the air. Cooper and Nora composed themselves and dutifully tried to get into the spirit of things, but whenever they glanced at one another they started laughing again.

Luckily, Maia apparently decided that they'd all gotten to know the wind well enough, and she led them back to the hotel, where they trooped into a large room filled with couches and comfortable chairs arranged around a big fireplace. Cooper gratefully removed her jacket and plopped onto one of the couches. Nora sat beside her.

"Maybe there will be cocoa after all," remarked Cooper hopefully.

But there was no cocoa. Instead, Maia asked them all to form an almost-circle facing the fireplace, where a fire crackled merrily. Maia sat in front of the fire, an acoustic guitar resting on her lap.

"Now that we've encountered Air a little bit, we're going to create our first song," she informed them. "This path is about discovering the creative energies inside of us. I hope your energies have been awakened by the air. Now I'd like you to let them out."

"We're going to write a song?" asked a woman across the circle from Cooper.

"That's right," said Maia. "As a group. It will help us learn to work with one another."

"But I've never written a song," the woman objected.

Maia shook her head. "It doesn't matter," she said. "This path is all about opening yourself up to the possibilities of creation. Try not to think in terms of what you haven't done or what you can't do or what you're afraid to do. That's the kind of thinking that blocks us. Just give this a try. You might surprise yourself."

"How do we do it?" a man a few people down from Cooper asked.

"I want you all to think about how the air felt,"

Maia replied. "Think about how it made you feel. Just throw out words or phrases that come to mind."

There was silence as the people in the circle thought for a while. Cooper, who had written a lot of songs, knew what they were probably thinking. They were embarrassed. They thought that what they were thinking was stupid and that people would laugh at them if they said what was on their minds. She'd felt stupid the first few times she'd written songs with other people. But she knew that the best way to get ideas flowing was to just start, so after a minute she said, "I felt like I was being tickled."

Her suggestion was met with laughter, and she knew that she'd broken the tension that people were feeling. Maia nodded her head. "Good," she said, writing Cooper's suggestion in a notebook beside her. "What else?"

"I felt like the Goddess was whispering to me," said a woman, smiling shyly.

"Great," Maia told her enthusiastically.

"I pictured faeries dancing around us," someone else suggested.

"I pretended I was flying," said another.

People threw out their suggestions more and more quickly, as if a dam holding back their ideas had been opened. Cooper listened to them, nodding at some and wondering where others had ever come up with their thoughts.

"I wonder if this is how Celine Dion writes all her songs," Nora said quietly so that only Cooper could hear.

Cooper knew what she meant. Some of the suggestions were a little bizarre. But it was fun to see people getting into the process, and as it went on Cooper found herself feeling the way she did whenever she started to write herself. There was a sense that something magical was happening, that within the list of ideas that Maia was scribbling down were the seeds of a song waiting to be born. Not all of the ideas she was hearing were good ones, but she knew that getting everything out was the important part. The bad ideas were just as important as the good ones.

Nora sat beside her silently, listening to what other people were saying. She herself didn't say anything for quite a while. Then, during a lull in the talking, she suddenly spoke up.

"I felt like I was being held in a giant frozen hand," she said. "It was like some invisible thing was squeezing the breath out of me."

Cooper looked over at the other girl. There was a faraway look on her face, as if she were remembering a dream she'd had or thinking about something sad. Then, suddenly, she shook her head and the old mischievous grin came back. "I was also hoping my hair wasn't getting *too* messed up."

A ripple of laughter went around the room, and Nora looked at Cooper, her eyes sparkling.

"Look out, Celine," Nora said.

"These are all great ideas," Maia told them. "We have a lot of things here. Now let's start putting the song together. I'm going to read out the list of things you all suggested. Concentrate on finding the strongest image. That's the one we'll use as the central theme."

She began to read back the different things that people had suggested. Cooper listened carefully, looking for the one thing that jumped out at her as being the most powerful image for a song. She wondered what other people would choose. *As long as it's not the faeries, I think we're okay,* she thought grimly.

Maia read through the entire list. Then she looked at the group expectantly. "Well?" she asked. "What do you guys think?"

Again no one spoke, and again it was Cooper who finally broke the silence. "I like the image of the wind being the voice of the Goddess," she said. "I think we can do a lot with that."

Maia nodded. "I like that one, too," she said. "What do the rest of you think?"

No one objected to the suggestion, and no one suggested anything better, so Maia decided that they would go with the idea. "Now we have to start writing," she said.

"But we don't know what the tune is," a man said. "How do you write a song with no music?"

"You don't need the tune," Cooper said, forgetting that she wasn't running the group. "You write the lyrics and then work it together with music." She looked at Maia, who was watching her. "Sorry," she said. "I didn't mean to interrupt."

"No, it's okay," Maia said. "It sounds like you know a lot about this."

"I'm in a band," Cooper told her. "I've written lots of songs."

"Why don't you help me out, then?" Maia suggested. "Can you play?" She held up the guitar.

"Yeah," Cooper said. "I play."

"Come on, then," Maia said. "I'm actually not very good. I could use someone who knows what she's doing."

Cooper hesitated. She was reluctant to take center stage. She was supposed to be a student in the path, not a leader. She'd never taken a leadership role in any kind of ritual apart from the ones she did with Kate and Annie, and she wasn't sure she knew what to do. *But you do know how to play the guitar*, she told herself. *That's all she's asking you to do.*

"Go on," she heard Nora say. "Go for it."

Cooper looked at her. Nora gave her a thumbs-up. Cooper grinned. "Okay," she said.

She stood up and walked to the center of the circle. Maia handed her the guitar and Cooper strummed it to see if it was in tune. She adjusted it slightly. Then she waited for Maia to continue. But Maia looked at her. "How would you do this?" she asked, smiling encouragingly.

Cooper thought. "I guess I'd come up with a

chorus first," she said. "That's the part most people hear and remember."

She played around on the guitar for a minute, humming to herself as she ran over some lyrical ideas in her head. She knew everyone was watching her, and she was a little embarrassed. But pretty soon the words took over and she forgot everything else. A minute later she sang, "She talks to me in wind and rain, she talks to me in storms. I hear her voice in rustling leaves and in the bending corn."

She paused, waiting for a response. People were nodding and looking at her approvingly. "It kind of takes the idea of the Goddess's voice being in things that are stirred by the wind," she said when no one spoke.

"I like it," a woman said. "It's like the air is the breath of nature and the breath of the Goddess. And I like that you talked about storms, because the Goddess isn't always calm and nice, you know?"

People laughed and nodded in agreement. "Let's work with that," Maia suggested. "Take the idea that the Goddess has moods and that those moods are reflected in how the air and wind behave."

Now that they'd gotten a jump start, people started coming up with all kinds of ideas. They threw them out one after another, and again Maia wrote them down. Then Cooper helped them organize their scattered thoughts into verses. Before too long they'd come up with the first finished one. Cooper read it to the group and watched their expressions change from doubt to elation at the realization that they'd just written something that actually sounded good.

"We wrote that?" asked the woman who had made the suggestion about faeries. "It's *good*."

"See what happens when you just let go and allow yourselves to create?" Maia said happily. Then she looked at her watch. "Let's take a break now," she said. "We'll meet back here in half an hour and work on the song some more."

People stood up and stretched, talked to one another, and wandered off in search of coffee or other things to eat and drink. As the room emptied, Cooper remained behind. She wanted to work on some music to go with the lyrics, so that she could surprise everyone when they got back.

"You did really well," Maia said to her.

"Thanks," said Cooper. "I wasn't sure how it would go, to tell the truth. I don't usually work well with groups."

"Well, you should think about doing more of it," replied Maia. "You're a natural teacher. I bet you'd make a wonderful ritual leader."

She smiled at Cooper and went to talk to some other people. Cooper sat with the guitar, playing and thinking about what Maia had just said. Her a natural teacher? No one had ever said anything like that to her. As she strummed on the guitar, picking out a melody, those words kept playing over and over in her mind. Teaching others was not something she'd ever considered. But maybe Maia was right. Maybe she *did* have something to share with people.

But right now she had a song to write. She stared at the lyrics they'd come up with and tried out different things musically, seeing what fit the words the best. She had several ideas, and she needed to play with them all before she decided on anything.

"You're a regular Bob Dylan," Nora said, making Cooper look up.

"I prefer to think of myself as an Aimee Mann," responded Cooper. "You know, the independent woman's voice and all. But I'll take Dylan, too. Thanks."

Nora sat down and watched Cooper play. "I wish I knew how to play," she said.

"It's actually not that hard," said Cooper. "You just have to keep at it. I started when I was pretty young, so now it's just what I do."

"Lucy can play," Nora said. "Yet one more thing she thinks she's better at than I am."

Cooper laughed. "No offense," she said, "but your sister seems a little gloomy. What's with that?"

Nora shook her head. "She takes everything *way* seriously," she replied. "She always has. I know we're twins and everything, but sometimes I can't believe we actually came from the same egg."

Nora was silent for a while as she listened to Cooper play. Then she said, "So, have you seen the ghosts?"

"You mean in the room?" asked Cooper. She

shook her head. "Not a peep out of them."

"You don't sound like you're all that worried about it," Nora said.

Cooper laughed. "Let's just say I've met enough ghosts so that they don't scare me."

"Really?" Nora asked. "You've seen ghosts?"

"I grew up with one," said Cooper. "And earlier this year I sort of helped one find the guy who murdered her."

Nora's eyes went wide. "You're kidding?" she said.

"No," Cooper said. "I know it sounds freaky, but it's true."

"I've never met anyone else who actually talked to a ghost," Nora said.

"What do you mean, anyone else?" Cooper asked her. "You've talked to one?"

"Yeah," said Nora.

"The ones in the room?" Cooper asked.

"Not the ones people think are in there," Nora said. "A different one."

Cooper raised an eyebrow. "You mean there are more than just the dead honeymooners?"

Nora nodded. "Way more," she said. "Lucy doesn't believe me, but I think you'll understand."

Nora looked as if she wanted to tell Cooper more about the subject, but before she could say anything else the others started returning to the room. Nora looked at them and said to Cooper, "We'll talk later."

CHAPTER 5

"You are all going to die."

Annie stared at Ginny. The older woman was sitting on the opposite side of the circle the group had formed on the floor of the room they were meeting in. The Earth path had attracted fewer participants than the other groups had, so the circle was fairly small. There were perhaps twenty people in it. Of those people, Annie was definitely the youngest by many years, and she was feeling a little out of place. It wasn't making her feel any more comfortable that the people around her were all laughing at Ginny's comment. How could they laugh about dying?

"I'm not being metaphorical when I say that," Ginny told them. "You are all going to die. This week. In class."

The laughter faded out as people realized that Ginny was serious. When they had all composed themselves, Ginny continued. "Winter is a time of death," she said. "The light fades and darkness takes over. The cold kills the plants and even some of the animals. Water freezes. For many of us, winter is like descending into death, and we can't wait to awake in spring and feel the warmth of the light again."

As Ginny talked, Annie couldn't help but think about her parents. The ten-year anniversary of their deaths was approaching. To her surprise, she realized that for the first time since the fire she'd almost forgotten about the approaching date. She had begun to heal during the year, thanks mostly to her involvement in Wicca, and the day of her mother's and father's deaths wasn't quite the looming specter that it had been for her in years past.

She hadn't been thinking about her parents when she'd chosen the Earth path. It had just seemed like a natural choice. But now that she was there she realized that, once again, something was pushing her into confronting her fears about death. She sighed. *I thought this was supposed to be a vacation*, she told herself. But magic didn't always work that way, she knew. Sometimes it snuck up on you and made you go places you had no intention of going. This, apparently, was one of those times.

"Most of us fear death." Ginny's voice brought her back to the moment, and she concentrated on listening to what the group leader was saying. "I know I do, and I'm closer to it than most of you."

Nervous laughter erupted from the circle. Annie knew that what Ginny said was probably true. After all, she was much older than most of them. But Annie also knew that death didn't necessarily take the oldest first. Sometimes it took people who had no idea it was coming for them, like her parents. Still, she understood that most people didn't want to think about dying before they were very old. She knew she would prefer not to. But there she was, thinking about it.

"Fearing death isn't anything to be ashamed about," said Ginny. "It's fearing it too much that prevents us from living. So this week we're all going to get dying out of the way. Then you won't have to worry about it again—I hope for a long time." She smiled at all of them, and Annie felt genuine warmth and love in the way she looked at the people gathered around her. It made her feel a little more relaxed, but she was still apprehensive. What had Ginny meant when she said that they were all going to die? What exactly was going to happen?

"We'll discuss the details as we go along each day," Ginny said. "But basically we're going to take a trip to the underworld. At some point this week, each of you will die. You will then journey to the land of the dead."

She let her words sink in, her eyes moving around the circle as she scanned the faces looking back at her. Then she said, "And you will come back again. As I'm sure all of you know, witches believe that we all return again and again to live in this world and enjoy it in different ways. Personally, I love that idea. So we're going to work with that, although I'm taking some liberties with the idea."

Ginny pointed to a row of tables set up at one end of the room. Annie had seen them when she came in, and had wondered what they were for. Now she waited to find out. Ginny indicated half a dozen large cardboard boxes that sat on the tables.

"In those boxes are the materials for making masks," she said. "We are each going to make a mask that symbolizes what it is we'd like to come back as after we die. We will then use those masks in our ritual, although I'm not going to tell you everything about it now. Today all you have to think about is what you would like to come back as. Then we'll make masks to represent those things."

"Does the mask have to be something specific, like a person or an animal?" asked a man to Annie's right.

Ginny shook her head. "Not at all," she said. "It *can*, if that's what you want, but it doesn't have to. It could just symbolize some personality trait you want to have. It can be as specific or interpretive as you like, as long as it really reflects what it is you hope to return as after your visit to the land of the dead."

All around the circle people nodded in understanding. Ginny clapped her hands. "Let's get started, then," she said. "To the boxes!"

They all stood up and went to the tables. People gathered around the different boxes and opened them. There were exclamations of surprise and excitement as they pulled out the contents. There were feathers and sequins and paints, scraps of material and sticks and seashells. All kinds of items came out of the boxes and found their way onto the tables. Annie stared at it all, her mind swirling with ideas as she tried to decide what she wanted her mask to look like.

"Take one of these," Ginny said, walking around with plain face masks and handing them out. "Use them as the basis for your masks. Glue things on them or paint them or do whatever you feel moved to do. You can't do it wrong."

Annie took the mask that Ginny handed her. Then she sat down and put the mask in front of her. She stared at it, thinking of it as her face. What did she want it to look like? The only mask she'd ever made had been a hedgehog head she'd fashioned out of papier-mâché for the Midsummer ritual she'd attended with Kate and Cooper. But that had been pure fantasy. This was serious. If she could be anything she wanted to be—anything at all—what would it be?

"I don't suppose coming back as Julia Roberts is an option, do you?" Ivy asked Annie as she took the seat next to her.

Annie laughed. "I think one Julia Roberts is enough," she said.

Ivy sighed, running her hands through her cropped brown hair. "Pity," she said. "We look *so* much alike. What are you going to make?"

Annie shook her head. "I really don't know," she said. "It's not every day that someone lets you pick what you come back from the dead as. I feel like I need to make it something really spectacular."

"I wouldn't worry too much about being spectacular," Ivy told her. "I don't think most of us *really* come back as Cleopatra or Madonna or anything quite so thrilling. After all, if we assume that who we are now is just the latest in a long line of people we've been, we have to assume the next time around will be kind of the same, don't you think?"

Annie shrugged. "I'm not sure what I think about it at all," she said. "What if when we're dead we're just dead?"

Ivy shuddered. "I don't like to think that's true," she said. "But I know what you mean. There are days when I think it would be nice to just have a good long rest. Star says that when she comes back she wants to be one of our dogs because all they do is sleep and eat and chase the goats around. That sounds pretty good to me sometimes."

"I wouldn't want to be a dog," Annie said firmly. "Nothing that has to eat out of a bowl and have forced baths."

While she knew what she didn't want to be, she still didn't know what she did want to be. She looked around the table to see what other people were doing, and was perturbed to see that everyone else seemed to be going at their masks with great enthusiasm. Unlike her, they weren't hesitating. They took things from the piles and worked with them, gluing and painting and decorating their masks. Even Ivy, after another moment of thinking, reached for some fake leaves in gorgeous fall colors and began to arrange them on her mask base.

Annie stared at the blank white face of her mask. It looked like a ghost, she thought, something without any real personality or form. It was waiting for her to bring it to life. But how? She closed her eyes and tried to picture herself with a different face. What would it look like?

Suddenly she had an image of sunflowers. Bright yellow sunflowers with dark brown centers. She knew where the image came from—a painting her mother had done of the flowers growing in their garden in San Francisco. But it was more than that. The flowers reminded her of light and the sun in all its glory. It was an image that made her recall the smells of summer and the way it felt to lay on the ground and feel the warmth of the grass and the earth beneath it. To her, sunflowers were strong and joyful, and that's what she wanted to be, whatever else she was in her next life. She didn't know what form she might take, but she wanted to be someone filled with the power of the earth and the sun.

Now that she knew what she wanted, she worked quickly. She had once seen an image of a Green Man, a face made up of leaves and vines. She had been drawn to it because of the way it seemed to be nature in human form, and that's what she wanted to do with her mask. She wanted it to look like a woman made of flowers, a face composed of petals and leaves. She looked around the table, seeing what there was she could work with.

She spied some deep gold paper, which she took, and some soft brown yarn, which she also scooped up. Then she started making her flowers. The petals were easy. She cut them from the paper and made a pile of them. But the centers of the flowers were going to be harder. She knew what she wanted to do, she just wasn't sure it would work right.

She unraveled the yarn and looked at it for a moment, thinking. Then she had an idea. Holding the four fingers of her left hand together, she wrapped the yarn around them about a dozen times. Then she slipped the loops of yarn from her hand, folded them in half, and wrapped some more yarn around the place where the loops were folded. The loose loops stood up, bound together into a tight bunch. Then Annie used scissors to snip the closed ends open, so that the lengths of yarn puffed out. When she was done, she held in her hand a dark brown mop of yarn that looked like the soft, dark center of a sunflower.

She took the center she had made and arranged some of the petals around it. It looked okay, but there was something missing. The flower appeared flat and lifeless, and she wanted to capture the beauty of a living flower.

"The petals need to stand up," Ivy suggested, looking at Annie's handiwork. "The centers are great. Now the petals need to be just as exciting."

Annie nodded in agreement. Ivy was right. But how was she going to make flat paper look like real, moving petals? She looked around the table, and saw a package of pipe cleaners. They gave her an idea, and she leaned over to pick them up.

Laying a pipe cleaner on the table, she took two of the golden petals and put glue on one of them. Then she laid the pipe cleaner down the center of it and placed the other petal over it, pressing them together. She let it dry for a moment and then tried bending the petal. It worked perfectly, the pipe cleaner acting as a framework to bring the petal to life.

Annie cut out some more petals and then went to work sandwiching the pipe cleaners between them. Before long she had a good-sized pile of them. She then made some more of the brown centers. When she was done, she started assembling the flowers. Cutting a piece of heavy paper into the shape of a circle, she glued the ends of the petals to it so that the petals spoked out like the rays of a sun. Then a brown center was glued to the middle of it, covering up the ends of the petals. After a little bending of the pipe cleaners, Annie had a gorgeous sunflower.

"Beautiful," said a woman across from her, who had been gluing shells to her mask and who was now painting blue swirls on them.

"I just have to make about fifteen more and I'll be all set," Annie said, wiping some glue from her fingers.

She spent the rest of the morning doing just that, and by the time lunch rolled around she had all the sunflowers made. After eating one of the sandwiches brought in by the hotel staff for them to munch on, she started assembling her mask. She'd made some green leaves out of paper and pipe cleaners as well, and she arranged the sunflowers on the mask with some of the leaves between them.

When she'd glued a few of them on, she held up the mask and looked at it. It really did look beautiful, and she was pleased with her work. Although she'd been doing a lot of painting since discovering that she shared some of her mother's artistic talents, she still never thought of herself as being all that creative. But the mask made her think that maybe she was, and looking at it filled her with a sense of accomplishment and pride. She was even more pleased to notice that some of the other participants were pointing over at her and nodding their heads appreciatively.

"I think you're a hit," Ivy told her.

"I'm just glad it's not a mess," Annie said.

After another hour or so she was finished. The sunflowers were glued all over the mask, with two small spaces left so that she could see out when she put the mask on. Looking at it, Annie could easily imagine that it was the face of a woman who had emerged from a field of sunflowers, stepping from between the rows and reaching her arms up to the welcoming sun.

"I see that most of you are done," said Ginny. She'd been walking around the table, looking at the different masks and talking to their creators. "Why don't we form a circle again? Bring your masks with you."

The class participants picked up their masks and returned to their seats on the floor. Annie sat with the others, cradling her sunflower mask in her hands.

"Look around at what your pathmates have done," Ginny told them. "You're each holding the face of your new self in your hands. See what you've each chosen to become."

Annie looked around the circle. Like her, the others were holding the masks in their hands facing out, so that the masks looked like faces peering back at her. Seeing them all, she was amazed at how creative people had been. They had come up with all kinds of ways to use ordinary objects in extraordinary ways, and the results were haunting and spectacular.

"You've created magic in these masks," Ginny said. "Now let's go around the circle and tell everyone what the masks represent."

The woman to Ginny's left went first. She held up her mask, which depicted a clown's face painted in bright, childlike colors. "I often feel like I don't play enough," the woman said. "I'm so busy and so worried about making sure everything goes smoothly for everyone around me that I have a hard time enjoying myself. So when I come back I want to be more playful and more carefree. Clowns represent that to me."

The man beside her showed them a mask with feathers sticking out all over it. "It's supposed to be an eagle," he said. "I guess it kind of looks more like a chicken."

People laughed, and the man smiled. "I just like the idea of being able to fly," he said. "Eagles are so free, and that's how I want to feel."

They continued around the circle. Each person had something to say about her or his mask, and Annie liked hearing why they'd chosen what they had. One man had made a mask with antlers, while another woman, who told them that she was suffering from a disease that was terminal, had made a mask featuring long flowing hair and healthy pink cheeks. She said that all she wanted in her next life was to be healthy, and to her the mask represented how she used to look and feel about herself.

Masks like that one made Annie sad. Others made her laugh and feel happy. When it was her own turn to show off her mask she held it up and sighed. "I don't have any particular story to go with this," she said. "To tell the truth, I don't really know why I picked sunflowers. I guess because they're pretty and they make me feel good. But I've been studying Wicca all year, and one of the things I've learned is that you should go with what you feel. My heart said sunflowers, so I made sunflowers. Maybe I'll figure out why when we do the rest of our rituals, but for now I just like the way they symbolize light and the earth."

The remaining people in the circle spoke after Annie. When they were done, Ginny nodded approvingly. "These masks are beautiful," she said. "They represent your strengths and your dreams—even if you don't exactly know what those are," she added, looking at Annie and smiling. "Annie's right that many of you will find out that your masks mean more than you know they do right now. The rituals we're going to do will bring out meanings that will probably help you understand why you chose the images you did."

Ginny paused, then continued. "We're going to end for the day now," she said quietly. "But tomorrow some of you will die. I can't tell you which ones, because I don't know myself. But some of you will die. So tonight you should all prepare yourselves for death, in case you're chosen tomorrow."

Annie looked around the circle at the faces of her pathmates. She barely knew them, and already some of them were going to die. But what did that mean, exactly? She wished that Ginny would be more specific about what was going to happen. But she also knew that not knowing was part of the overall experience.

Maybe you'll be one of the ones who dies, she told herself. The thought troubled her. She looked down at the mask in her hands. Suddenly, the bright sunflowers didn't make her feel good at all.

CHAPTER 6

"We had the *best* time," said Sasha as she emerged from the bathroom, drying her hair with a towel. "Luna is the coolest. We spent all morning doing yoga, and then in the afternoon we did this weird interpretive dance stuff to some Goddess music she had." She paused to take a breath. "So how did your paths go?"

"Mine was kind of intense," Annie said. She wanted to show her friends the mask she'd made, but Ginny had collected them all and taken them away. Annie wasn't sure why, but Ginny had told them that they'd be getting them back later and not to worry.

"Mine was fun," Cooper said. She was sitting on her bed, playing the guitar that Maia had loaned her. She was still working out the details of the song they'd worked on all afternoon. "One of those twins is in the same path as me. Nora. She's really cool."

"Well, her sister isn't," Kate remarked. She was getting dressed, and was checking her appearance in the big mirror that hung on the wall. "Lucy's in my path, and she's a real downer."

"Did you have to work with her?" Annie asked.

Kate shook her head. "No," she said. "But she kept shooting me these weird looks. I think there's definitely something wrong with that girl."

"Nora said that Lucy is a little off," Cooper commented. "She also told me that there's a ghost around here," she added.

"We already knew that," said Sasha, pulling a T-shirt over her head.

Cooper shook her head. "This is a different ghost," she said. "She didn't get a chance to tell me much about it, but she said that Lucy doesn't believe her about it."

"Feuding twins," Sasha said. "How fun. I can't imagine not liking someone who looked just like me. It must be weird."

"I'll find out more later," Cooper said. "Right now, let's go eat. I'm starving."

The four girls finished getting ready and then went downstairs for dinner. When they arrived they went through the food line and then sat at a table with Sophia. They were joined by Thatcher, one of the men from the Coven of the Green Wood, and Thea.

"Did everyone have fun in path today?" Thatcher asked when they were seated.

"I don't know if *fun* is the best word for it, but yeah," Annie replied.

"Right," Thatcher said. "You're in Earth. I hear some of you are dying tomorrow."

"What does that mean, exactly?" asked Annie.

Thatcher exchanged looks with Sophia and Thea, then gave Annie a blank look. "I have no idea," he said, trying desperately to sound sincere.

"You are *such* a bad liar," replied Annie. "But that's okay. I'm sure I'll be able to handle it."

Thatcher laughed. "I'm sure you will," he said.

"Where do you guys go all day?" Cooper asked him. "I don't see any of you in our classes."

"We have our own path," Sophia explained. "It's for people who have been teachers in the past."

"And what do you guys do?" Kate inquired.

"Very secret stuff," answered Thea. "We can't talk about it."

"She means they sit around telling bad stories," said Tyler as he arrived at the table. "Mind if I join you?"

"Not at all," Thatcher told him. "Here you go."

Thatcher patted the empty seat beside him, which also happened to be next to Kate. Tyler pulled out the chair and sat down. Kate gave her friends a startled glance but didn't say anything.

"You guys have all taught here before?" Annie asked Sophia, Thea, and Thatcher.

"Several times," Thatcher answered. "If you come often enough, they rope you into it."

"Maybe you'll teach here one day," suggested Sophia thoughtfully. "Cooper, I hear you already did a little bit of teaching of your own in your path."

Cooper blushed. Had Maia been talking about her to the others? Part of her was horrified to think so, but another part of her was secretly pleased.

"I just helped out with writing a song," Cooper said. "It wasn't a big deal, and I wouldn't say it was teaching."

"That's what teaching is," Thatcher told her. "Showing people how to do something. Don't sell yourself short."

For the rest of dinner they talked about their paths and about what they'd done. Then a bell rang and they saw Bilbo standing at the front of the room.

"Hello again," he said. "I hope you all had wonderful first days."

There was a burst of applause and whistling as people indicated their satisfaction with the day's activities. Bilbo waited for it to die away, then continued. "As we have every year, we're going to use the evenings for informal classes and socializing. Anyone who wants to can offer a class, and this is the list." He held up a piece of paper with some writing on it. "If you want to offer a class, just write your name on here along with what the class is, what time it's meeting, and where," Bilbo explained. "And if you want to take a class, just check out this list and see what interests you. It will be posted on the door to the dining room."

He walked through the dining room and taped

the list to the door. People got up from their tables and went to see what was on the paper. The girls, intrigued, joined the crowd around the list. When they got close enough to read it, they scanned the list.

"Ooh," Sasha said. "Past life regression. That sounds like fun."

"Not for me," Cooper remarked. "I have enough problems with *this* life. I don't want to know about the past ones."

"What about palm reading?" Annie said. "Could be fun."

"Or trance techniques," Kate suggested.

"How about a ghost hunt?"

The girls turned around and saw Nora standing behind them. "Hey," she said.

"A ghost hunt?" Annie asked her. "Are you serious?"

Nora nodded. "I told Cooper a little bit about it earlier today," she said. "You guys interested?"

Annie looked at the others. "What do you guys think?"

"It's better than this other stuff," remarked Cooper.

"Can you guarantee a ghost?" asked Sasha doubtfully.

"Not definitely," Nora admitted. "But I can try."

The four girls looked at one another. "Okay," Cooper said. "We're in. What do we do?"

"Meet me at the east tower in an hour," Nora

told them. "That's the one at that end of the hotel," she added when they all looked at her blankly. "Go to the top floor and wait by the door at the end of the hall. I'll meet you there. I just have to take care of some stuff first."

She was looking at something behind them. When they turned to see what it was, they saw Lucy staring at them. She gave Nora a cold look and turned away.

"What's with her?" Sasha asked.

"Nothing," said Nora. "Just ignore her. Meet me in an hour, okay?"

"Sure," Annie said. "We'll be there."

Nora left them, and the four girls went to the lobby to see what was going on. There they sat on one of the couches and talked.

"I'd really love to know why Nora and Lucy seem to hate each other," Annie said. "That look Lucy gave us was really hostile."

"Who knows why people do half the things they do?" Sasha said. "Maybe it's one of those good twin, bad twin things like in the movies. You know, Lucy is the psychotic one who tries to poison people with arsenic, and Nora is the normal one."

"You really watch way too much television," Cooper teased. "Next thing you know, you'll be telling us that Nora is trying to lure us to our deaths."

"Oh, that's good," Sasha said thoughtfully. "Yes. She's telling us we're going on a ghost hunt, but really she's going to take us to a deserted part of the hotel and lock us in. Perfect."

Cooper threw a pillow at her, which Sasha caught and threw back. They were all laughing. Then Annie said softly, "Don't look now, but the evil twin is watching us."

They all looked. Lucy was standing in a doorway across the lobby from them, watching them intently. But when she saw them turn their gazes in her direction, she quickly turned and ran away.

"Good going," said Annie. "I said not to look."

"You can't tell people not to look and expect them not to look," Cooper said indignantly. "That's like saying, 'Here comes that cute guy you have the big crush on. Oh, by the way, pretend not to notice.'"

"Great," Sasha said. "Now she knows we're on to her and her wicked ways. I bet she tries to off us in our sleep now."

The ridiculous comment drew another round of laughs, and pretty soon they forgot all about Lucy. Then Kate looked at her watch. "It's time to meet Nora," she said. "Let's go."

They got up and walked down the hallway. When they reached the stairs, they climbed to the fourth floor and then walked to the end of the hallway. Just as Nora had told them, it ended at a door, which was locked. A moment later Nora herself appeared. She produced a key from her pocket and held it up.

"If my father knew I had this he'd kill me," she

said as she fitted the key into the lock.

"Why?" Cooper asked her. "What's the big deal about this door?"

"We just don't use the room in the tower," explained Nora. "He doesn't like us to come up here."

"But this is where the ghost is?" Kate said.

"Last time I saw her it was," said Nora, pulling the door open.

"Her?" Annie repeated. "It's a her?"

"Yes," Nora said as she motioned for the others to go through the door.

Cooper went first. As she stepped through the door she flipped the electrical switch on the wall and a dim light went on somewhere above them, illuminating a staircase that spiraled up. Cooper began walking up the stairs.

"It looks like no one has been here in years," she said, running her finger over the dust on the railing.

"They haven't," confirmed Nora, stepping in after Kate, Sasha, and Annie had passed through the door. She pulled the door shut carefully behind them.

"What were you doing up here, then?" Sasha asked. "I mean, if your parents declared it off-limits and all."

"Isn't that reason enough?" Nora asked, grinning.

"Yeah," Sasha agreed. "But I bet there's more to it than that."

"There is," said Nora. "I found a diary."

"A diary?" said Annie.

"It belonged to a girl who used to live here," Nora explained. "Her name was Mary O'Shea. She died here."

"Died how?" asked Kate.

"That's what I don't really know," Nora answered. "The diary only goes so far. Then it ends. But I did some research and found out that Mary died not long after she stopped writing the diary. She wrote a lot about coming up here, which is why I came here."

They reached the top of the stairs, which opened up into a large room. It was big and empty, with a plain wooden floor and windows looking out in all directions.

"This doesn't look like anything special," Kate remarked as they gazed around at the barren space. "What did she do up here?"

"I think she just wanted to be alone," Nora answered. She was walking around the big room, touching the walls gently and speaking in a soft voice. "I think she felt safe here."

"When did her ghost appear to you?" asked Cooper.

"About a year ago," Nora replied. "I was up here late one night. I think it may have even been a full moon. I'd brought the diary with me and was reading it. I heard a noise, and when I turned around she was standing there." She pointed to a spot in front of one of the windows. "At first I was terrified, but there was something about her that made me not be afraid. So I talked to her."

"She spoke?" said Annie. "What did she say?"

"She just told me that her name was Mary and that she had lived here," said Nora. "It was like she couldn't remember any more than that. After a while she just kind of faded out."

"That sounds familiar," Cooper said. "Elizabeth Sanger, the girl who haunted me, did the same thing at first."

"But that was because she had died so violently and suddenly," Annie reminded her. "When did this girl die, Nora?"

"In 1873," Nora answered.

"And you said you don't know how it happened?" asked Kate.

"No," Nora said. "I found a newspaper clipping, but all it said was that she died."

"It could have been anything," Cooper said. "We should try to find out. That could be why she's appearing to you."

"This is so cool," Sasha said. "I've never seen a ghost before."

"It's something else, all right," Annie assured her, thinking of the few times it had happened to her.

"How many times have you seen her?" Cooper asked Nora.

"Maybe half a dozen," she answered. "But never for very long. She just shows up sometimes."

"Do you think we can make her appear?" Annie asked Cooper.

Cooper shrugged. "It's worth a try," she replied. "Are you guys up for it?"

"Count me in," Sasha said instantly.

"Kate?" Cooper asked.

Kate nodded. "Yeah," she said. "Okay."

"Let's stand in a circle and hold hands," suggested Cooper. "We can try to call to her."

The five girls arranged themselves in a circle in the center of the room, holding hands. Cooper took a deep breath. "We should cast a circle," she said.

"What for?" asked Nora.

"For protection," Kate explained. "It keeps us surrounded by positive energy."

"Oh, but Mary isn't dangerous," Nora said. "She's a good ghost."

"It's not about her being good," said Annie. "Whenever you invite another entity in you should set up a barrier in case it brings any kind of negative energy with it."

Nora frowned. "Okay, I guess," she said. "But I don't think you need to do it."

"Everyone imagine white light flowing out of our hands and forming a circle," Cooper said.

They stood in silence for a minute as they created a circle with their energy. Then Cooper said, "The circle is cast. We are in sacred space. Nothing may enter uninvited, and all within the circle are safe from harm. Now let's call to Mary. Nora, maybe you should do it since you're the one who has seen her before."

Nora nodded. "Okay," she said. "I'll try. But like I said, she doesn't always show up." She took a few deep breaths. Then she said, "Mary O'Shea, we call you. If your spirit is near, please show yourself."

The five of them stood in the room in silence, waiting for something to happen. When the light suddenly went out, they let out little shrieks of surprise.

"We must have blown a fuse," Cooper said.

The moon, only a few days past full, was shining brightly outside, so the room was still dimly lit by its light. It was enough to see in, so they remained in their circle, waiting for something else to happen. Minutes went by with nothing more occurring. Then a voice said, "I'm Mary O'Shea."

The girls looked and saw a figure standing by one of the windows. It was a girl. She appeared to be around their age, but she was dressed in old-fashioned clothes. She wore a long white dress tied with a bow in back, and her long hair was tied back with a ribbon. Her face was pretty, and she looked at them with eyes that showed no fear.

"Mary!" Nora said. "You came."

"Yes," Mary said. "I came. I heard you calling me."

"These are my friends," Nora said excitedly.

"What do you want with me?" Mary asked, ignoring Nora.

"We want to help you," Annie said as Mary turned

to look at her. "We want to know how you died."

Mary cocked her head, as if thinking. "I was killed," she said.

"But how?" Cooper asked. "Who killed you?"

"Someone close to me," said Mary sadly. "Someone very close to me."

"Who was it?" Sasha asked anxiously.

Mary looked up again. This time she smiled sadly. "I must go," she said. "Good-bye."

"Wait," called Cooper.

But Mary's ghost was already fading away, and a moment later the place where she had stood was nothing but empty space with moonlight shining on the wall.

"She's gone," Nora said sadly.

"Yes," Cooper said. "But she came, and she spoke to us. We can probably get her to come back again."

"And we know a little bit more," said Annie. "We know someone killed her."

"But we don't know who it was," Sasha said.

"Maybe there's a clue in the diary," Kate suggested. "The one you found, Nora. Can we see it?"

Nora shook her head. "I don't have it anymore," she said. "I lost it."

Kate sighed. "Too bad," she said. "That would have been really helpful. Well, we'll just have to wait until we can talk to her again."

"Thanks for trying, anyway," said Nora. "I appreciate it."

"I don't understand why Lucy doesn't believe you about Mary's ghost," Cooper said. "Why don't you just bring her up here and show her?"

Nora snorted. "Lucy only believes what she wants to believe," she said.

"Well, we believe you," Cooper said. "And we'll do whatever we can to help you."

Nora smiled. "Thanks," she said. "I really appreciate that. I'm so glad you guys came."

"We should probably get out of here now, though," said Annie. "But we'll be back."

"Oh, yes," Nora said. "I know we'll be back."

CHAPTER 7

"Yesterday you told someone your greatest fears," Jackson said to his group on Monday morning. "But you didn't know who that person was. Today we're going to do something different. We're going to work with partners again, but this time you're going to know who your partner is because there will be no blindfolds."

Kate felt a knot forming in her stomach. She really wasn't big on partner exercises. The day before had been difficult enough, especially considering what her partner had told her. It still freaked her out a little bit, especially since she still had no idea who she had been paired with. But the idea of talking face-to-face to someone she didn't know about personal things made her feel even more nervous.

"I know choosing partners can be awkward," Jackson said. "So I've made it easy for you. I've written numbers on pieces of paper and put them into the cauldron." He indicated the small cast-iron cauldron that sat in the center of the circle and had been the focus of a lot of attention since they'd gathered in the room that morning. "Each of you will choose a number. Then you just have to find the other person who has the same number. That person is your partner."

"But you haven't told us what we're going to do," a man said. Kate was secretly relieved to hear that he sounded almost as nervous about the exercise as she was.

"All in good time," said Jackson. "Numbers first."

Everyone stood up and walked to the cauldron. Kate hung back as other people selected their pieces of paper. Somehow she figured that would postpone the inevitable, although she knew that was ridiculous. Several other people were standing back from the main group as well, and Kate noted gloomily that one of them was Lucy. The girl seemed even more depressed than she had the day before, and Kate couldn't help but remember how Lucy had been spying on her and the others after dinner. *She was probably up all night thinking of ways to make us miserable*, Kate thought.

Finally the crowd cleared away from the cauldron and Kate stepped forward to select a number. She snatched a piece of paper and stepped away. Opening it, she saw the number 13. *How perfect*, she thought, sighing.

"Okay," Jackson said, looking into the cauldron.

"You should all have your numbers now. Go find the person who has the same number."

Kate looked around. People were busily comparing numbers or holding up their papers for everyone to see. One by one the matching numbers found one another and pairs formed. She was disheartened to see that no one was coming toward her or looking at her. She'd sort of been hoping that someone she knew would have her number. But the only person she knew was Star, and she was paired with a young man wearing a Mickey Mouse T-shirt.

Soon there appeared to be no one left. Kate looked around but didn't see anyone else who appeared single. She walked up to Jackson. "I think maybe I'm the odd one out," she said, more relieved than anything that perhaps she wouldn't have to partner with someone.

"No," Jackson said. "There are definitely an even number of people. Someone doesn't have a partner." He took Kate's number and looked at it. "Number thirteen," he called out. "Is there another number thirteen?"

"That would be me."

Kate looked around and saw Lucy standing a few feet away, clutching a piece of paper in her hand and looking unhappy.

"I'm number thirteen," she said.

"Great," said Jackson jovially. "Then you girls are partners for today. Why don't you go get settled."

Kate looked at Lucy, who looked down at her

feet. *Of all the people*, she thought as she walked toward the other girl. But there was nothing she could do about it.

Lucy didn't look at Kate as they walked over to an empty area of the room and sat down. Kate ignored her, looking at Jackson as he gave them their next instructions.

"This morning's exercise is about sharing yourself with others," Jackson said. "It's also about listening. What we're going to do is play interview. Each of you will get ten minutes to find out as much as you can about the other person. Then you'll switch roles and your partner will find out as much as she or he can about you. When both of you have had a chance to do the interviewing, we'll come back in a circle and you'll be asked to share a little of what you've learned. So decide which of you is going to ask questions first. We'll begin in one minute."

Kate looked at Lucy, who was still not meeting her eyes. Did she really have to find out anything about this girl? she wondered. She couldn't imagine that the two of them would really have anything to talk about. She would have very much preferred to be interviewing the other twin instead. Nora was so much more outgoing, and Kate couldn't help but wish that Cooper was the one saddled with Lucy.

"I guess I'll go first and interview you," Kate said when Lucy showed no sign of wanting to participate in making the decision. *At least then I'll get it out of the way*, she told herself as Lucy nodded silently.

"All right," Jackson said. "We're beginning now. When ten minutes have gone by I'll let you know and you can switch."

Kate looked at Lucy. What should she ask? She really didn't know.

"What's your favorite color?" she asked stupidly, resorting to the one thing she could think of.

"My sister took you up there, didn't she?" Lucy said unexpectedly. She was looking at Kate now, and Kate saw that she had the same intense eyes as her sister, only Lucy's radiated fear, where Nora's shone with self-confidence.

"She took you there, didn't she?" Lucy repeated.

Kate nodded. "Yes," she said. "But I don't see what the big deal is. She's right, you know. About the ghost, I mean."

To Kate's surprise, Lucy responded by laughing softly. "Of course she's right," she said. "Why wouldn't she be?"

Kate wrinkled her brow. "But she said that you didn't believe her about the ghost," she said.

"Oh, I believe her," Lucy replied. "I've seen her, too."

"Then why won't you help her?" asked Kate, getting angry as she thought about poor Mary and how sad she'd seemed. "She needs your help."

Lucy put one of her fingers in her mouth and chewed on the nail. Glancing at Lucy's hands, Kate could see that all of her nails were bitten down to almost nothing. "Is that what she told you?" Lucy asked, peering into Kate's face.

"No," Kate said. "Mary told us herself. We asked Mary's ghost to appear and she came."

"Did she tell you about how she died?" asked Lucy.

"She said she was killed by someone who knew her," Kate said. "Look, why are we talking about this? We're supposed to be finding out about one another."

"This is important," Lucy said.

"If it's so important, why can't you talk to us about it instead of hiding and spying on us?" asked Kate.

Lucy looked away. She scanned the room as if she was making sure that it was safe to talk. Then she looked back at Kate.

"Mary isn't who she says she is," she said.

Kate shook her head. "She's a ghost," she said. "How can she not be who she says she is?"

"Did Nora tell you about the diary?" asked Lucy in a low voice.

"Yes," answered Kate. "But she said she lost it."

Lucy let out a sound like the beginning of a laugh, but she stopped herself. "She didn't lose it," she said. "I took it. I burned it."

"But why?" asked Kate. "That diary could be the clue to Mary's death. It might tell us who killed her."

Lucy's eyes narrowed and became very clear.

"Nora knows who killed Mary," she said. "She knows."

"What are you talking about?" snapped Kate, getting angry. "She doesn't know. If she knows, why would she need us to help her find out?"

"I don't know," Lucy admitted, looking away. "She's planning something."

"Yeah," said Kate. "She's planning on helping a dead girl find some peace. But you seem determined to prevent that. I don't get it. What's wrong with you?"

"Your ten minutes are up," Jackson called out before Lucy could answer Kate. Kate just sat there, looking at the other girl. She wanted an answer. But Lucy wasn't saying anything. She was just looking at the floor. Then she looked up and into Kate's eyes.

"What's your favorite color?" she asked.

Kate glared at her. How could Lucy just change the subject like that? There she was, claiming that Nora was somehow lying to them about Mary, and she wouldn't explain herself. Kate wanted answers, not questions. She wanted to know what Lucy had meant when she said Nora knew who killed Mary; she wanted to know about the diary. Why would Lucy have burned the diary? But Lucy showed no sign of saying anything else. She just sat there, looking at Kate with her empty eyes.

"Blue," Kate said.

Neither of them said anything for the remainder of their time together. They just sat, looking anywhere but at each other. When Jackson finally called an end to the exercise, both Kate and Lucy got up and walked quickly back to the circle. They took seats as far away from one another as possible.

"Now we're going to go around the room and say what we learned about our partners," Jackson said. "Just tell us one thing that you think is the most important of all the things you learned during your interview."

Kate only half listened as the other people in the group spoke. She was still thinking about her exchange with Lucy. Something about it bothered her, something beyond all of the weird things that Lucy had said about Nora and the ghost of Mary. It was something Kate couldn't quite put her finger on, but it was hanging around like a melody she'd heard but couldn't recall in its entirety.

"Kate, what did you learn about your partner?"

Kate looked up, startled to hear Jackson speaking to her. She hadn't been paying any attention. Now, apparently, it was her turn to talk. But what could she say? She hadn't learned anything about Lucy, really. But everyone was looking at her. She had to say something or she'd look like an idiot.

"Oh, um, I learned that my partner is a twin," she said. It was the only thing she could think of to say about Lucy. At least, it was the only thing that wasn't mean. "I learned that my partner is delusional" wouldn't really cut it, even if it was what Kate would like to say.

Jackson nodded. "That's a start," he said. "Next time try to find out more about your partner's personality, though, and not just the surface things. It's important to learn how to really listen to what people are saying."

Kate nodded, feeling herself turn red. She knew that saying that Lucy was a twin was stupid. But what else could she say? And what could Lucy possibly say about *her*? She hadn't asked Kate about anything except her favorite color, and saying that Kate's favorite color was blue would be even stupider than Kate's saying that Lucy was a twin. *At least someone will look dumber than I did*, Kate comforted herself.

Eventually, Jackson got around the circle and came to Lucy. When it was her turn she looked up and said, "I learned that my partner trusts people too easily," she said clearly, looking right at Kate.

Kate felt herself growing angry. She wanted to stand up and deny what Lucy had just said. Then she reminded herself that probably no one even remembered who had partnered with whom. No one was looking at her, she noticed. No one except Lucy, who continued to stare at her in that irritating way she had.

How dare she? Kate thought bitterly. *She made that up because she wanted to make me angry. She doesn't know anything about me. Nothing. She didn't even ask me any questions.*

"That's an interesting observation," Jackson said to Lucy. "That's the kind of thing I was hoping would come out in the interviews. It shows that you really got your partner to open up to you. Good work."

Hearing Jackson praise Lucy, Kate got even madder. Lucy hadn't gotten her to open up. She hadn't done anything at all except make some wild accusations about her sister.

Sister. The word suddenly resonated in Kate's mind. She looked at Lucy, who was once more looking at the floor. *Sister.* She'd been talking about her sister. *Of course,* Kate thought. *Why didn't I realize it before?* Like the answer to a math problem's suddenly coming clear, Kate realized what had been nagging at her. *I'm afraid my sister is going to kill me.* The words came back to Kate as if she'd just heard them. And now she knew *whose* voice had spoken them. It was Lucy's. The voice yesterday had had the same dead tone to it that Lucy's did. There was no mistaking it now that the connection had been made.

She really is crazy, thought Kate. Not only was Lucy saying all kinds of ridiculous things about what Nora had told them and what they'd seen with their own eyes, but she wanted Kate to believe that Nora was trying to kill her. Now Kate almost felt sorry for her. How could she believe something so absurd? Kate tried to imagine Nora hurting anyone, let alone her own sister, and she knew that it just wasn't possible.

"Well, I think this exercise was a great start to the day," Jackson said when the last person had spoken. "You've learned a lot about each other."

We sure have, Kate thought, glancing at Lucy and thinking about everything she had to tell the others when she saw them later that afternoon. *We sure have*.

CHAPTER 8

"Psst."

Cooper looked around to see where the hissing sound was coming from. At first she thought it was just one of the hotel's old clunky radiators rattling. But when the sound came again, she looked harder for the source. She found it in the form of Kate, who was standing in the doorway looking at her with a strange expression. When she saw Cooper looking at her, Kate motioned for her to come to the door.

"Why didn't you just come in?" Cooper asked her friend. "We're on break anyway. It's not like you're interrupting anything."

"I don't want Nora to see me," Kate said, dragging Cooper into the hallway.

"Nora?" Cooper said, sounding confused. "Why wouldn't you want her to see you?"

"Something weird happened in path this morning," explained Kate. "Lucy said some stuff about Nora and Mary."

"What kind of stuff?" asked Cooper.

Kate shook her head. "It's all crazy," she said. "She said that Nora knows more about Mary's death than she's telling us. She said she took the diary from Nora and burned it. She said that Nora knows who killed Mary and that she's planning something."

"Planning something?" Cooper said. "Did she say what?"

"No," said Kate. "She said she doesn't know what it is."

Cooper sighed. "This all sounds like some desperate attempt to get your attention," she said. "She says these vague things and doesn't really give you any details."

"There's something else," said Kate. "She thinks that Nora is going to kill her."

Cooper rolled her eyes. "Right," she said slowly. "That's *definitely* what's going on. How could we not notice? Kate, this girl is clearly insane."

"I know," replied Kate.

"Then, why are you telling me this?" Cooper asked.

"I don't know, really," answered Kate. "Just so you know what's going on, I guess."

"You don't believe her, do you?" said Cooper.

"No!" exclaimed Kate. "I think she's making it all up just to get attention, like you said." She paused. "But maybe Nora *does* know more than she's telling us about Mary's death."

"Why would she hide something from us?"

Cooper said. "She wants to help Mary, remember?"

"Like I said, I don't know," said Kate. "I don't think she's keeping anything from us either. But maybe there's something she doesn't think is important. I just don't think we should overlook anything."

Cooper nodded. "You're right," she said. "I'll see if I can get Nora to remember anything else. Thanks for telling me about Lucy. I'm sorry you're the one she's dumping on, though."

Kate snorted. "It's just another challenge, right?" she joked.

"I've got to get back," said Cooper. "I'll talk to Nora and see what I can find out. I'll see you later this afternoon."

Kate left, and Cooper returned to the room where the others were taking their lunch break before getting back to work.

"Where'd you disappear to?" asked Nora, walking up with a soda in her hand.

"Oh," Cooper said. "Bathroom break. Say, I've been thinking a lot about Mary and what's going on."

Nora opened her soda and took a sip. "And?" she asked.

"Well," said Cooper, "I'm just wondering if maybe there's something you're forgetting about."

"Like what?" Nora asked her. "I told you everything I know."

"I know," Cooper said. "But maybe there's something you're overlooking. You know, something that doesn't seem important to you but that might be really important."

"I don't know what it could be," replied Nora.

"Maybe we should start at the beginning again," Cooper said, sitting on a couch and motioning for Nora to sit next to her. "Tell me everything."

Nora sat down. "Like I told you, I found Mary's diary."

"Where did you find it?" asked Cooper, interrupting.

"I was cleaning out one of the rooms," answered Nora. "It was one of the ones we hadn't redone yet. There were some loose boards in the floor, and when I moved one of them I found the diary underneath it."

"And what kind of stuff was in the diary?" Cooper inquired.

Nora shrugged. "Just the usual girl stuff," she said. "She wrote about what was going on at the hotel, and about her friends. It was pretty boring, actually. Oh, and she wrote about this guy she had a crush on. That was probably the most interesting thing. He was a gardener here at the hotel."

"Sounds pretty routine," said Cooper. "You said she used to spend a lot of time in the tower room. Do you know what she did there?"

"I think she just wanted to get away," answered Nora.

"From?" Cooper asked.

"Her family," Nora replied. "You know how it is

when you're a teenager."

"Oh, do I," Cooper said, grinning. "Now, you said that you don't know anything about how she died, right?"

Nora nodded. "I've never found out anything about that," she said.

"She was really young," Cooper said thoughtfully. "It had to have been an accident of some kind."

"That's what I think," said Nora. "But then she said that she was killed, and by someone who knew her."

"We need to find out more about her death," Cooper said. "Is there anyone who might know something?"

"Not that I can think of," Nora answered. "It was a long time ago."

"And you've never asked your parents about it?"

Nora shook her head. "No," she said. "Like I told you, they wouldn't be too thrilled if they knew I'd been hanging around up in that room—especially if I told them I'd been talking to a ghost."

"But they seem so cool about this kind of stuff," said Cooper.

"They are, mostly," Nora agreed. "But I think the idea of the hotel's being haunted is easier for them to accept than knowing that it's *really* haunted, if you know what I mean."

Cooper thought about her own house, which was haunted by the ghost of its original owner. The story about the ghost was a big draw for the tourists who flocked to the historic house for tours, but when Cooper had actually seen it as a child her mother had been less than thrilled about it. "I know what you mean," she told Nora.

"Can we all come back together?" Maia was standing in the center of the room, motioning for them to recircle.

"We'll talk about this more tonight," Cooper told Nora. "And don't worry, we'll figure out what happened to Mary and help her do what she needs to do."

"I know you will," Nora said, squeezing Cooper's hand. "And thanks."

"Any time," Cooper told her. "Now, let's go see what's next on our agenda."

The girls joined the others in the circle. They had finished their song that morning, and Maia had hinted that they would be doing something really fun for the afternoon session. Now she stood in the center of the circle with a mysterious smile on her face.

"We're going to play a game this afternoon," she said. "Yesterday we wrote a song based on our interactions with the element of air. That went really well, thanks especially to Cooper."

Several people applauded, and Cooper found herself blushing. Then Maia continued. "Today we're going to do something else designed to help you release your creativity. Only instead of writing a song, we're going to write a story."

There were groans from some of the class members, and Maia fixed them with a look. "You didn't think you could write a song, either," she said. "And look how well that came out. A story is just another way of using words."

"What are we supposed to write about?" asked Nora.

"That's the fun part," Maia answered. "You're each going to write the first half of a story. It can be about anything you like, as long as it's a couple of pages long. Then we're going to exchange those first halves with each other and you're going to write the second half of someone else's story."

"How can you finish someone else's story?" asked one of the men.

"By using your imagination," Maia explained. "This exercise challenges you in several ways. First, you have to come up with a story that someone else can take over and do something with. Second, you have to take what someone else has started and finish it. Then we're going to read the stories to each other and see what you've all come up with. Now, get started. You have an hour to write your first halves. Then we'll switch and you'll spend another hour finishing the stories. And then we'll have the readings."

Cooper opened her notebook and took out a pen. "Do we have to sit here to do this?" she asked.

"No," Maia said. "You can go anywhere you want to, as long as you're back here in an hour."

Cooper nodded, then turned to Nora. "I'm going to go work on this somewhere else," she said. "I can't write with other people around."

"Okay," Nora said. "I'm going to stay here."

"See you in an hour," Cooper said, getting up.

She left the room and walked down the hallway. She felt bad about lying to Nora. She *could* write with other people around. But there was something she wanted to do, and she didn't want Nora to know she was doing it.

Cooper walked through the lobby to the front desk. She was relieved to see that neither Bryan nor Fiona Reilly was working the desk. Instead, a perky-faced girl she'd never seen before was standing there.

"Hi," Cooper said when she reached the desk. "Um, I was wondering if you could help me with something?"

"Sure," the girl said chirpily. "What is it?"

"Well, I'm really interested in the history of the hotel," Cooper told her. "I was wondering if you have any literature about it or anything."

The girl frowned. "You know, we sure don't," she said, sounding disappointed.

"That's too bad," Cooper replied. "I was hoping to find out a little bit more about it."

"Well, you could ask the Reillys," the girl suggested. "Their family has owned it since it was built."

"Oh, I don't want to bother them," said Cooper

hastily. "I know they're really busy and everything. Thanks anyway, though."

She started to walk away when the girl called her back. "There's someone else who might know something," she said. "Old Mr. Greaves."

"Who's he?" asked Cooper.

"He's one of the caretakers," the girl told her. "He's been here forever. He's a little cranky, but if anyone is going to know anything, it will be him."

"Where can I find him?" Cooper asked her.

"Try the basement," said the girl. "He's usually down there fussing around with the furnaces and stuff. Just go through the dining room and then down the stairs at the back. You'll find it."

"Thanks," Cooper said. "I'll go look for him."

She left the lobby and walked through the deserted dining room. Next to the entrance to the kitchen she found the stairs leading to the basement, and she went down them. She found herself in a long hallway. Pipes ran over her head, and the air was much warmer than it was upstairs. Every so often she heard something rattle as water or steam passed through a pipe.

She walked down the hall, following the pipes overhead, until she came to a large room. A row of furnaces sat at one end of it, and just as the girl at the desk had predicted, there was a man walking around them. He was checking the instruments and occasionally giving one or another of the furnaces a whack with a wrench he carried in his hand. Cooper approached him carefully, not wanting to startle him.

"Excuse me," she said. "Are you Mr. Greaves?"

The man turned around and fixed her with a look. He really was old. His skin was wrinkled, and what hair he had left was almost pure white. He looked at Cooper suspiciously. "Who wants to know?" he growled.

"The girl at the desk told me I could find you here," Cooper said. "I'm one of the guests."

"Guests aren't allowed down here," the man said. "I've got work to do."

He turned around and went back to inspecting the furnaces. But Cooper wasn't about to give up so easily, so she tried again.

"The girl said that you might be able to tell me something about the history of the hotel," said Cooper.

Mr. Greaves grunted but didn't say anything.

"I was hoping you could tell me something about Mary O'Shea," said Cooper.

Mr. Greaves stopped working on the furnace and turned around slowly. "Where did you hear that name?" he asked Cooper.

"So you know who she is?" Cooper replied, not answering his question.

Mr. Greaves nodded. "Of course I do," he said. "The question is why *you* know about her."

"What can you tell me about her?" asked Cooper.

Mr. Greaves looked at her appraisingly before

laughing. "You're not going to tell me how you found out about Mary, eh?" he said. "Well, good for you. I like that."

Cooper grinned at him. "Okay," she said. "Let's just say that someone told me a little something about her and I want to know more."

One of the furnaces hissed, and the old man turned to peer at it suspiciously. "Damn things have been acting strange all day," he said, turning a dial on one of them. Then he turned back to Cooper. "Mary O'Shea lived in this hotel," he said. "Her parents ran it. She died on the evening of her sixteenth birthday."

"Do you know how?" asked Cooper.

"She fell," said the caretaker. "From the east tower room."

"But how could she fall from there?" asked Cooper. "There's no balcony or anything."

Mr. Greaves looked at her curiously, and Cooper knew he was wondering how she could know what the tower room looked like. For a moment she thought he was going to question her further, but then he just nodded. "There used to be a walkway around it," he said. "The O'Sheas had it removed after their daughters died."

"Daughters?" Cooper said. "There was more than one?"

"Mary had a twin sister," said Mr. Greaves. "Alice."

"And how did she die?" Cooper inquired.

"Same way her sister did," answered the old

man. "She fell from the tower."

"I'm confused," Cooper said. "How did they both fall from the tower?"

"They fell together," Mr. Greaves said simply. "They died together."

Cooper stared at him. "There were *two* girls who died that night?" she asked. "And they were twins?"

"No one knows how it happened or why they were up there," Mr. Greaves said in reply. "They found them in the snow, holding on to one another like they were sleeping."

Cooper tried to take in this new information. If it was true, why was only Mary appearing to Nora? Why wasn't Alice's ghost haunting the tower room? Then Cooper remembered what Mary's ghost had said. She had been killed by someone close to her. Could it be Alice?

But why? Cooper wondered. *Why would one sister kill the other?*

"Is there anything else you want to know?" Mr. Greaves asked Cooper, bringing her back to the moment.

Cooper shook her head. "No," she said. "Thanks for telling me this."

"There are people who said that Alice and Mary O'Shea weren't quite right," said the old man.

"What do you mean?" asked Cooper.

Mr. Greaves shrugged his shoulders. "My grandfather told me that," he said. "He was the caretaker here when it happened. He found them, almost frozen. I remember him saying that a lot of people were afraid of the girls. They thought they had powers, that they could do things. Bad things. Some peculiar things occurred that year."

"Like what?" asked Cooper.

"A gardener died mysteriously," answered the caretaker. "Drowned in the pond. There were other things, but I don't remember a lot about it. My grandfather didn't like talking about the girls. No one did."

Cooper waited for him to say more, but he didn't. "Well, thanks again," she said. "I should be getting back upstairs."

Mr. Greaves suddenly looked straight at her. "Whatever it was that killed those girls, don't go stirring it up," he said. "Stay out of that room."

Cooper nodded. "I will," she said, knowing even as the words left her mouth that she was lying.

One of the furnaces gave a rumble, and Mr. Greaves turned his attention back to it. "I'm coming. I'm coming," he said, as if the machine were a person demanding that he come to its aid. "What's gotten into you today, anyway?"

Cooper left the old man to his work and went back upstairs. As she emerged from the basement she checked her watch. She had only twenty minutes to write her story. *Well, it will have to do*, she thought as she sat at one of the empty tables in the dining room and opened her notebook.

She wrote quickly, making up some ridiculous

story about a girl who answers the door one after-noon only to discover that there's a policeman standing on her front step. "Let someone else decide why he's there," she thought as she finished up and closed the notebook.

As she walked back to the room where her path was meeting, she thought about everything Mr. Greaves had told her. There was definitely more to the story than Nora had told them—if she even knew it. But unlike the story Cooper had just writ-ten, the story of Mary and Alice O'Shea had an end-ing. It was the beginning that was missing.

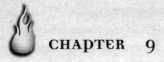

CHAPTER 9

Annie stood with her eyes closed, her hands at her sides. *I'm ready to die*, she told herself. *I'm ready to die*. She'd been repeating that to herself for the past few minutes, ever since Ginny had told them to stand in a circle and keep their eyes shut. Now the leader was walking around the circle, speaking in a gentle voice.

"Today some of you will die," she said. "Are you ready? If you should feel the hand of death on your shoulder, will you go willingly?"

Suddenly, Annie heard a gasp from somewhere in the circle. What had happened? She almost opened her eyes, but Ginny's voice prevented her from doing so.

"Those of you who are chosen should step forward," she said.

Annie waited to feel a hand on her shoulder. She had already made up her mind that she was going to be chosen, and now she was just waiting for confirmation of that fact. It was a strange feeling. She knew that none of them were *really* dying, but still she was apprehensive. What would this dying mean? What was going to happen to them? Ginny hadn't given them any clues.

"Death has chosen." Ginny's voice was clear and firm. "Open your eyes."

Annie opened her eyes and looked around. Half of the class members were standing inside the circle, while the rest of them remained where they had been, looking at those whom death had selected. Annie was surprised to discover that she hadn't been chosen, and even more surprised that she wanted to cry with relief.

"Those who have died, turn and look at those who are living," instructed Ginny.

The "dead" turned and faced the people who had not been tapped on the shoulder. Looking at their faces, Annie wanted to cry all over again. Among them she saw Ivy looking back at her, her eyes damp. How did it feel for her to be one of those who had died?

"The dead will now choose one of the living to help them make the journey from this world to the next," Ginny said. "Please select a partner, someone you feel can best care for you as you pass over."

The people in the inner circle looked around, searching the faces of those facing them. One by one, they stepped forward and took one of the "living" people by the hand. Annie was happy when Ivy stepped forward and took her hand.

"Will you help me?" she asked.

Annie nodded, unable to speak because of the lump in her throat. The older woman squeezed her hand gently, and Annie choked back tears. There was something very touching about the way Ivy had come to her, and although Annie had no idea what would happen next, she found herself wanting to comfort Ivy.

"What we are going to do now is prepare the dead for their journey to the underworld," Ginny informed them. "We will do this by creating a death mask for each of them."

Annie looked at Ivy quizzically. "What does she mean?" she asked.

Ivy shook her head. "Got me," she said.

"On the tables you will find towels and mask kits," Ginny continued. "Each kit contains a bowl of water, some plaster bandages, and a small jar of petroleum jelly. Each of the living should take a kit. Then take your dead and find a quiet place in the room. We'll continue from there."

Annie left Ivy and went to the table. Sure enough, she discovered that there were plastic bowls of warm water and boxes of bandages and petroleum jelly. She took one of the kits, along with a towel, and returned to Ivy.

"Where would you like to go?" she asked.

"How about over by the windows?" Ivy asked her. "I like the light there."

They walked to their chosen place and sat on

the floor. All around the room other pairs were doing the same. When they were all seated, Ginny said, "Now we will make our death masks. The dead should lie down. The living will then prepare the mask by first smoothing a thin layer of petroleum jelly over the face and neck to keep the bandages from sticking to the skin. Once you've done that, you will take the plaster bandages. One at a time, dip them in the water and smooth them over the face of the dead. Don't get them too wet, and don't apply them too tightly. Be sure to leave openings for the nose so that your dead can breathe, too."

There was nervous laughter from the class members at Ginny's comment. It seemed odd to Annie that she was telling them to make sure that "dead" people could breathe, and she laughed with the rest of them.

"Get started," Ginny said. "I'll come around and give you more directions individually."

Annie looked at Ivy. "Are you ready for this?" she asked.

"We'll find out," Ivy replied, stretching out on the floor.

Annie spread the towel over Ivy's chest, so that only her head stuck out above it. She opened the jar of petroleum jelly and scooped out a little. Then she began to gently apply it to Ivy's cheeks.

"Remember that you're preparing a body for burial," Ginny said as she walked among them. "The dead should not speak or move, and the living should really think of them as dead. Feel the face that you're touching. Think about the person it belongs to."

Annie looked at Ivy's face as she rubbed a thin layer of jelly over it. Her eyes were closed, and her lips were set in a peaceful smile. She looked like she was sleeping.

As her fingers caressed Ivy's face, Annie really looked at her. She'd only known Ivy for a short time, but she felt close to her.

Once the petroleum jelly was smeared evenly over Ivy's face, Annie wiped her fingers on the edge of the towel. Throughout the process, Ivy hadn't so much as moved a muscle. It really was as if she were dead, and Annie was even starting to think of her that way. A respectful silence had settled over the room, and it felt very peaceful and solemn. Annie looked around and saw the other pairs working quietly. She wasn't surprised to see that some of the participants were wiping their eyes or even crying openly.

"This exercise will bring up many emotions," Ginny said as she observed the teams. "That's okay. Cry if you need to. Allow yourself to feel. If you think it's getting to be too much, just raise your hand and I'll come to you."

Annie opened the box of plaster bandages. Taking one out, she dipped it into the warm water and then pulled it through her fingers to wipe off the excess water. She took the now-soft bandage and laid it across Ivy's forehead, smoothing it over her skin with her fingertips. The bandage conformed to the shape of Ivy's face like a second skin.

One by one, Annie took the bandages and laid them over Ivy's face. Slowly her skin was covered by the chalky white strips and the mask formed. Annie was careful not to let any of the water run down Ivy's neck, and she took extra time with the area around Ivy's nose. As the mask took shape, Annie wondered what it was like for Ivy to feel her mouth and eyes covered, to feel her skin encased like a mummy in the plaster bandages, which were very quickly drying and becoming hard.

From time to time Annie stopped to stroke Ivy's hair and to touch the portions of her face that were still uncovered. A calmness had come over her, a calmness mixed with deep sadness that grew deeper as more of Ivy's real face disappeared, replaced by the cold whiteness of the mask. As Annie laid bandages over Ivy's eyes, she remembered how brightly those eyes had sparkled. As she covered Ivy's mouth, she thought about the woman's carefree laugh. All of these things were gone now, hidden behind the bandages.

"That's wonderful." Annie looked up to see Ginny crouching next to her, watching her work.

Annie smiled at her, unable to say anything in response. She didn't want to talk and spoil the mood. More than that, she didn't know what she could possibly say. Preparing Ivy's death mask was turning out to be a totally different experience from anything she'd expected. She felt a sense of responsibility toward her, a responsibility to send her on her journey with as much love as she could.

"When you've completed your masks, sit with the dead and attend them while the masks dry completely," said Ginny.

Annie looked at Ivy's mask. It was finished. Her features were all covered by a blanket of white, the eyes blank and the mouth sealed shut. Annie put the remaining bandages and the bowl of water to one side and just sat beside Ivy. *What should I do?* she asked herself.

She began to hum quietly as she sat next to Ivy, her hand on the other woman's shoulder. She found that she was humming a familiar chant that they often used in rituals. *We all come from the Goddess*, she thought to herself as she hummed the tune. *And to her we shall return, like a drop of rain flowing to the ocean.* It seemed appropriate for the occasion, with its message of birth and death and rebirth, and she hoped that Ivy didn't mind her humming it.

After another ten minutes or so, Ginny called to them. "It is now time for the dead to journey to the underworld," she said. "Will you all help your dead to stand?"

Annie took Ivy's hand and held it as she sat up. Then Ivy stood, her masked face looking blankly out into nowhere.

"Put your hand on the shoulder of your dead,"

Ginny said. "And follow me as we travel to the land of the dead."

Annie placed her hand on Ivy's shoulder and put her other hand on her elbow. Ivy shuffled forward as Annie led her in the direction of Ginny. Ginny moved slowly as the masked "dead" followed her with their attendants. She led them to a door at the side of the room that opened out onto a snowy expanse of lawn. When they reached the door, Annie looked out and saw that paths had been shoveled into the snow. The paths spiraled around each other in a circular shape.

"This is the labyrinth that leads to the land of the dead," Ginny told them as they stood at the doorway. "Each of you will walk your dead through the labyrinth until you reach the center. There you will wait until all the dead have arrived."

The first pair stepped forward into the labyrinth. Annie watched as they made the first circle, moving carefully. They were followed by another pair, and then another. Then it was her and Ivy's turn. Still holding Ivy's elbow in her hand, Annie urged her forward and they stepped out onto the snowy path.

The afternoon air was warm and the sun was bright, but still Annie felt chilled as she and Ivy walked along the labyrinth's circular path. It was arranged in interlocking circles, so that from time to time they passed other pairs walking. Annie looked at the masked faces of the "dead" as they passed, and at the still-living faces of their attendants. Some were stained with tears, while others appeared peaceful and relaxed.

The journey through the labyrinth, as they made tighter and tighter circles, took about ten minutes. Then they reached the center. Annie guided Ivy to a spot beside another pair, and the two of them stood and waited for the other teams to finish their trips through the labyrinth.

When they were all in the center, Ginny appeared at the entrance to the labyrinth. "Attendants, you must now say your final good-byes and leave the land of the dead. You cannot stay there. You belong here in the land of the living. Quickly! Leave your dead and run back to me! Leave now!"

Annie found herself unable to move. Ginny's voice was so insistent, so commanding. And part of her didn't want to remain in the land of the dead any longer than necessary. But another part didn't want to leave Ivy there, all alone and with her mask on. How would she see? Who would help her? Annie couldn't just abandon her.

"Come back to the land of the living!" Ginny called again. "Come now! You don't belong in the land of the dead!"

All around her, other people were leaving their partners and running back through the labyrinth. The "dead" continued to stand there, their empty faces looking out as their attendants left them behind.

Annie knew she had to go. She gripped Ivy's hand tightly one last time and whispered, "Good-bye." Then she let go and ran after the others. As she circled the center she looked at Ivy, standing all by herself, and she felt the tears she'd been holding back run down her face. As she raced for the land of the living and left the dead on their little frozen island of snow, she let out all the emotions she'd been feeling during the mask-making process. Her heart was breaking, and it hurt.

She exited the labyrinth and stood with the others. Most of them were sniffling, and some were weeping openly as their friends and pathmates comforted them. A woman Annie had never really spoken to put her arm around Annie and hugged her. "It's okay," she said as Annie wiped her eyes.

When the attendants were all gathered outside the labyrinth, Ginny called to the people remaining inside it. "Dead, you are no longer with us," she said solemnly. "Turn your backs on the living and enter the other world."

Slowly, the masked people turned around so that their backs faced their attendants. They stood there, facing away, as the people outside the labyrinth watched silently. Annie looked at Ivy's back and felt her chest heave as she cried. It hurt so much to say good-bye, and she felt like she'd done too much of it in her life—first to her parents, then to her friend Ben Rowe. Although she knew that Ivy wasn't really dead, she felt as if she were. It reminded her of the ritual she'd participated in at Midsummer, when she had attended an actor playing the part of the Oak King and she'd watched him "die" during a mock battle with his brother, the Holly King. That had been hard, but this was harder. She wanted to run back through the labyrinth and embrace Ivy. She wanted to save her from dying. But she couldn't.

"The dead are gone from us," Ginny said to the assembled class. "They have gone to the land of the dead, where you, too, will go one day. But they will not stay there."

She turned back to the people in the labyrinth. "Take off your masks," she called to them. "Remove the faces of death."

Annie watched as the people in the land of the dead carefully removed their death masks. They put their fingers under the edges and loosened them, prying them off gently. Most of them held the masks in their hands and stared at them for a while. Then Ginny said, "It is now time to return to the land of the living," she said. "Come back to us."

One at a time, the people in the labyrinth turned and looked back at the others. They smiled, their faces shiny with the remnants of the petroleum jelly and bits of plaster. *They look so happy*, Annie thought, and the weight in her chest disappeared almost instantly.

"Put down your masks," Ginny said. "You don't need them anymore. Come, return to the land of the living and begin your new lives."

The people in the labyrinth laid down their masks and began the walk back through the maze. As each one emerged at the end, she or he was greeted with hugs and kisses by the people already there. Annie waited expectantly for Ivy to arrive, watching as she circled in the snow before stepping out. Ivy held out her arms, and Annie ran to her.

"Welcome home," Annie said.

"It's nice to be back," joked Ivy.

When everyone had returned from the land of the dead, Ginny led them back inside. There they discovered that while they were outside, the masks they'd made on the first day had been laid on tables.

"It's now time for the reborn to put on their new faces," Ginny said. "Take up your masks and put them on."

People went to the tables and found their masks. Putting them on, they looked at one another and laughed. There was something childlike and joyous about what they were doing, and the feeling was contagious. As Annie looked at the women and men donning their new identities and walking around, she was filled with happiness.

"You did such a good job," Ivy said to her, coming up to Annie after finding her leafy mask and putting it on. "I felt so loved and cared for. At first I was terrified. But as your fingers moved over my face, I actually felt at peace. And when you started humming I knew everything would be okay."

Annie hugged her friend. "I'm glad I could do it," she said.

"I just hope I can do as good a job for you tomorrow," said Ivy.

Tomorrow, Annie thought, realizing suddenly that the ritual wasn't over yet. *Tomorrow I die*.

CHAPTER 10

"There were *two* of them?" Sasha said in amazement as the girls sat in their room after dinner that night. Cooper had just finished telling them about her conversation with Mr. Greaves.

"That's right," replied Cooper. "Twin sisters."

"Just like Nora and Lucy," Annie said. "That's really weird."

"Why do you think Nora didn't say anything about it?" asked Kate.

"Maybe she didn't know," said Cooper.

"I find it hard to believe that Mary wouldn't at least *mention* her sister in her diary," Annie remarked.

"Annie's right," Sasha said. "She had to have known. Besides, if the O'Sheas really were related to the Reillys, don't you think she would have heard something about the story? I mean, it's kind of a big deal."

Cooper sighed. "I know it all seems strange," she said. "But I think we should give Nora a chance to explain before we get all excited."

"You haven't spoken to her yet?" asked Kate.

"No," Cooper said. "I didn't really know what to say. I asked her to meet us here in a few minutes. We'll do it then. But I don't want it to seem like we're ambushing her or anything."

"I wonder what Mr. Greaves meant when he said that the O'Shea girls made strange stuff happen," Annie mused.

"Maybe Nora knows something about that, too," said Kate.

There was a knock on the door, and they all looked at Cooper. "Here's our chance to find out," she said as she got up and opened it.

"Hey," Nora said, coming in and plopping down on one of the beds. "Are you guys ready to try and contact Mary again? I have a feeling that tonight we'll find out more."

"About that . . ." said Cooper. "We have some questions."

"Shoot," Nora said cheerfully. "I'll tell you what I know."

"Well, for starters, did you know that she had a twin sister?" Cooper asked.

"And that they both died in a fall from the tower room?" Kate added.

"How did you find out that stuff?" asked Nora, looking slightly concerned.

"I did some digging around," said Cooper vaguely. "I wanted to see if I could find out what happened to Mary, and that's what I found out. So, did you know about it?"

Nora rubbed her hands on her thighs. "Yeah," she said. "I guess I did."

"Why didn't you tell us, then?" asked Annie. "Why did you pretend you didn't know anything?"

Nora sighed. "Look," she said, "I'm sorry I didn't tell you. There's more to this story than I told you. But I didn't mean to hide anything. I guess I was just waiting for the right time to tell you all of it."

"Right time?" Kate echoed. "What does that mean?"

Nora looked down at her feet, as if she was thinking. Then she looked up. "I'm scared," she said. "I'm really scared."

Cooper shook her head. "I am *really* confused here," she said. "You told us that you wanted help contacting this ghost so that we could figure out who killed her. Now you're telling us that you're scared. What are you scared of?"

"Lucy," Nora said softly. "I'm scared of Lucy."

"Why are you scared of her?" asked Annie. "She's your sister."

Nora laughed ruefully. "Alice was Mary's sister, too," she said. "And she killed her."

"Alice killed Mary?" said Sasha. "I thought they fell."

"That's what everyone thinks," Nora said. "But that's not what happened. Alice pushed Mary."

"But Alice died, too," said Annie.

121

"Because she fell pushing Mary," Nora replied.

"Now I really don't get it," Cooper said. "Why would Alice kill Mary?"

"Because Mary knew what Alice was doing," Nora answered.

"Doing?" said Kate questioningly.

Nora paused before continuing. "Alice was involved in magic," Nora told them all. "Dark magic. She was using her powers to hurt people."

"Mr. Greaves mentioned that some weird stuff happened that year," Cooper said.

"That's what I mean," said Nora. "Alice had been using her powers to do bad things. Mary found out about it and tried to stop her."

"So Alice killed her?" Kate asked.

"She was desperate," Nora explained. "There was this guy—a gardener—who worked at the hotel. Alice was in love with him. But he loved Mary, and when he told Alice that she went crazy. She did this spell and made him drown. Mary didn't know at first. But she found out, and when she confronted Alice about it, Alice told her that she'd better be careful or she would be the next one to have an accident."

"How do you know all this?" asked Cooper.

"It was in the diary," Nora replied. "Mary wrote all about it."

"But the gardener drowned over the summer," Annie said, thinking about it. "The girls didn't die until December. Why did it take so long for things to explode?"

"Mary was trying to keep Alice controlled using magic," said Nora. "She made a talisman using her hair and hid it somewhere in the house."

"Sympathetic magic," Kate said. "We certainly know how *that* works."

"We had a little run-in with a Ken doll once," Annie explained to Nora, who nodded.

"As long as Mary had the talisman, Alice couldn't hurt her," Nora continued. "But then Alice found the talisman. She destroyed it, and she made an even more powerful one to use against Mary. Mary searched all over the house, but she couldn't find it anywhere. Finally, in desperation, she went to the tower room to perform one final ritual, one that would break Alice's spell over her. But Alice showed up. They fought, and Alice pushed Mary from the ledge. Only at the last second Mary grabbed Alice's hand, and she fell, too."

"That last part couldn't possibly be in the diary," Annie said. "Mary couldn't have written it before she died. How did you find out about it?"

"Mary told me," said Nora.

"Okay," said Sasha. "So now we know what happened. But that still doesn't explain why you didn't tell us any of this before."

"I had to be sure I could trust you," said Nora. "I knew that if you offered to help Mary that I could count on you."

"Count on us for what?" asked Kate.

"To help me fight Lucy," Nora responded.

"Now we're back to Lucy," Cooper said. "What does she have to do with this?"

"Lucy has been talking to the ghost of Alice O'Shea," said Nora. "She started doing it about a year ago. Alice has been telling her all kinds of lies, and Lucy believes them. I've tried to make her see that it's not right, but she won't listen to me."

"What has Alice been telling her?" asked Kate.

"She's promised Lucy that she'll show her how she can gain incredible powers," answered Nora.

"Powers?" asked Sasha. "What do you mean?"

"Both Lucy and I have always kind of been able to do things," Nora replied. "You know, little spells and stuff. Ever since we were kids. But Lucy wants to do more. Alice told her that she'll help her do that if Lucy helps her."

"Helps her what?" said Annie.

"That's what I don't know," Nora answered. "Mary doesn't know either. But she says we have to hurry."

"But hurry and what?" said Cooper. "If we don't know what Alice is trying to do, how can we hurry?"

"We can help Mary come back," Nora said.

"Come back?" said Sasha.

"Just for one night," said Nora. "The Winter Solstice. That's the night they died. If Mary can come back to our world on that night, she says she can make sure that whatever Alice is planning on doing is stopped and that the two of them will move on to the spirit world."

"But how do we help her come back?" Kate asked.

"We have to find the talisman that Alice made," Nora told her. "It's still hidden somewhere in the house. If we can find it, then Mary can come back and do what she needs to do."

Cooper sighed. "I think maybe we should talk to Sophia about this," she said.

"No!" Nora said emphatically. Then, when she saw everyone looking at her, she said more calmly, "I don't think that's a good idea. She'd want to tell my parents, and I don't want them to know what Lucy has been doing. Even though she's done some awful things, I still hope I can stop her from doing anything stupid and get her back to normal."

"She told me that she's afraid you're trying to kill her," Kate told Nora.

"What?" said Nora, sounding shocked. "She told you that?"

Kate nodded. "In path the other day."

Nora shook her head. "She's been getting worse," she said, sounding worried. "You've seen her. She used to look normal. Now she looks like some kind of goth freak or something. I have no idea what Alice has been doing to her, but we have to help her."

"Lucy also told me that she stole the diary," Kate said.

"So that's what happened," Nora said. "I should

125

have known. I thought I lost it. Did she say what she did with it?"

"She told me she burned it," replied Kate.

A shadow fell across Nora's face when she heard Kate's news. "She burned it?" she repeated.

"That's what she said," answered Kate.

"I can't believe she told you all of this," Nora said. "Why would she do that?"

"Maybe to throw us off the track," suggested Cooper. "If she doesn't want us helping you, the best way to do that is to make it look like you're the one who's up to something."

Nora put her face in her hands. "I wish you guys could have seen her before all of this started happening," she said. "She used to be so happy and fun to be around. Then she got mixed up with Alice's ghost, and everything changed."

"Now that we know what's really happening, what's the game plan?" Sasha asked.

Everyone looked at Cooper, who always seemed to have a plan. She thought for a minute. "You say that the talisman Alice made to control Mary is still in the house somewhere, right?" she asked Nora.

"That's right," Nora replied. "Or at least Mary thinks so, because it wasn't destroyed before Alice pushed her from the tower. Besides, she's been trying to come through into our world for a long time and can't, so something is holding her back. She believes it's the talisman."

"Then we have to find the talisman," Cooper said. "And apparently we have to find it before the night of the Winter Solstice."

"And you have no idea what it is that Lucy and Alice are planning for that night, right?" asked Cooper.

"No idea," Nora answered. "But I'm sure it's bad, whatever it is. Alice had grown very powerful before her death, and Mary says she's very anxious to get back into our world to finish what she'd started."

"Today is the nineteenth," Cooper reminded them all. "That gives us less than forty-eight hours to do this."

"Where do we even start?" Kate asked. "This place is huge. The talisman could be anywhere."

"Nora, you have to think," said Cooper. "There must have been some clue in the diary, some mention of a place that Alice liked to go. My guess is that she hid it there."

"Believe me," Nora said, "I've thought and thought about that. I even went to the places Mary mentioned in the diary. But I couldn't find anything. Alice was smart. I think she would have hidden the talisman someplace where Mary would never think to look."

"Do you even know what it is?" asked Annie. "A talisman could take any shape."

"I know it was made with some of Mary's hair," Nora replied. "But I don't know what she made with it."

Sasha sighed. "This sounds pretty hopeless," she said. "We're looking for something, we don't even know what it looks like, and it could be hidden anywhere. Oh, and it's been over a hundred and twenty-five years since it was hidden, so we don't even know that it's still here."

Annie put her arm around Sasha. "Hey," she said. "We've had to do weirder things. Welcome to the wacky world of Wicca."

"Sasha's right, though," said Kate. "How *do* we start looking?"

"Why don't we start with the places we *don't* look?" suggested Cooper. "I assume that you've been looking for a while, right?" she added to Nora.

Nora nodded. "For a couple of months," she answered. "As soon as Mary told me what I was looking for, or at least as much about it as she knew."

"Then let's make a list of those places," said Cooper. She fetched her notebook from the dresser and opened it. "Start talking," she told Nora.

Nora began rattling off a list of locations around the hotel. Cooper wrote them all down as she enumerated each one. Nora continued for several minutes, and when she finally stopped Cooper looked at the list she'd made.

"Wow," she said. "You've been busy. You actually checked every room?"

Nora nodded. "We help clean them anyway," she said. "I just took a little extra time in between changing the sheets and washing the windows."

"But you didn't find anything?" Kate asked.

"Nothing," said Nora. "Except for a lot of spare change under the beds."

"The garden shed, the pool house, the kitchen, the library," Cooper read. "The ballroom, the billiard room, and the wedding chapel. That seems to pretty much cover everywhere."

"Trust me," Nora said, "there's more. This is a *big* hotel. But yeah, I covered most of it."

"This is really frustrating," Sasha remarked. "It's like looking for the needle in the haystack."

"Here's a thought," Annie said. "What if the talisman isn't hidden at all?"

"What do you mean?" asked Nora.

"I mean, what if someone has it already?" Annie said. "Someone like Lucy."

"That would be perfect," Cooper said. "Of course she would want it so that Nora couldn't find it and help Mary. And since Alice is the one who made it and hid it, she would obviously know where it was hidden."

"I bet that's it!" Nora said excitedly. "I bet she's had it all along! No wonder I couldn't find it anywhere." For a moment she looked triumphant, but then her face fell and she frowned. "But if she has it, we'll never find it," she said.

"Not unless she tells us where it is," Kate replied.

"Right," said Sasha. "Like she's going to do that."

"She would if she thought I believed her," said Kate slyly.

The others looked at her for a minute and then began grinning. "That's dirty," Cooper said. "I love it."

"Think about it," said Kate. "She's been giving me little hints for the past couple of days. Obviously, she wants me to believe her story. So, what if I pretend to? I'll tell her that I've been thinking about it and that I want to help her. Once she thinks I'm sincere, I bet she'll tell me everything."

"You have to be careful," said Nora. "Lucy is dangerous right now. Alice has her all turned around, and she isn't thinking clearly. I mean, she thinks I'm out to get her. If she thinks for even one second that you're lying to her, I don't know what she would do."

"Nora's right," said Annie. "Remember what happened when we tried to pull one over on Sherrie last summer? Lucy is ten times smarter than Sherrie is. You're going to have to play this really cool, Kate."

Kate nodded. "Don't worry," she said. "I have a plan. By tomorrow night I'll have her eating out of my hand. That talisman is as good as ours."

Nora took a deep breath. "I sure hope so," she said. "Because if we don't get it, I don't know what's going to happen."

CHAPTER 11

The next morning, when Kate arrived at the room where the Water path was meeting, the first thing she did was look for Lucy. She saw the girl standing by the windows, gazing out of them with a peculiar look on her face. Taking a deep breath, Kate walked over to her, thinking, *Here goes nothing.*

"I need to talk to you," she said.

Lucy shot her a sideways look. "Why?" she said. "So you can think I'm even crazier than you already do? I don't think so. You've made your choice. You're on Nora's side."

"No," Kate said, shaking her head. "Not anymore. We asked her some questions last night and her story didn't check out."

Lucy looked at her again. This time there was a spark of hope in her eyes. "What did you ask her?" she said.

"Cooper found out some things," said Kate. "About Mary." She paused before adding, "And about Alice."

"You know about Alice?" Lucy asked, turning to face Kate for the first time.

"Yes," Kate said. "We know about the accident in the tower room."

"That was no accident," Lucy said.

"I know," said Kate.

Lucy studied Kate's face for a moment. Kate looked back at her, her gaze unwavering. She knew that if she showed the slightest sign of being nervous Lucy would know she was lying. She had to make the other girl think that she really was on her side now and not on Nora's.

"What else did Nora tell you?" asked Lucy, clearly testing Kate.

Kate swallowed. This was the make-or-break moment. "She told us about the talisman," she said. "The one Alice made to keep Mary from working any magic."

Lucy's eyes flickered for a moment before her steely expression returned. "Mary can't be allowed to come back," she said quietly. "If she does, everything will be ruined."

Kate nodded. "I know," she said. "That talisman is the key." She paused a moment before asking the question that was at the heart of her charade. "Do you know where it is?"

"Maybe I do," answered Lucy. "But why should I tell you where it is? As long as Nora can't find it and return it to Mary, everything is okay."

Kate and the others had anticipated this

response, and they had come up with a story they hoped Lucy would buy. "We think the talisman may be weakening," Kate told Lucy.

Doubt flashed in Lucy's eyes. "What do you mean, it's weakening?" she said breathlessly. "That talisman has worked for over a hundred and twenty-five years. Why would it weaken now?"

"I don't know," Kate told her. "But Mary's ghost is getting stronger, so something is happening."

Lucy looked away, staring out the window again. For a minute Kate thought that everything was over and that the other girl had decided she was lying. But then Lucy looked back at her. This time her eyes were sad.

"If I tell you where the talisman is, what are you going to do?" she asked.

"We'll try to strengthen it," answered Kate. "Cooper, Annie, and me. We've done a lot of magic, and we think we could add enough energy to the talisman to keep Mary's ghost from crossing back over."

"Mary is very powerful," Lucy told her. "It will take a lot to hold her back."

"We think we can do it," Kate said. "But we need that talisman if we're going to try."

"I don't know," said Lucy. "I have to think about it."

Inside, Kate groaned. Lucy was holding out on her. If she didn't produce the talisman, then Mary's ghost would be trapped and whatever Alice was planning would most likely take place on the evening of the Winter Solstice. There was also the risk that Lucy would tell Alice what the others were planning, and then everything would be ruined. They needed to get the talisman, and they needed to get it as soon as possible.

"We don't have a lot of time," Kate said, applying gentle pressure. "The longer we wait, the less time we have to strengthen the talisman."

Lucy nodded. "I know," she said. "I'll let you know as soon as I can. In the meantime, thanks."

Kate smiled. "It's okay," she said.

Lucy smiled crookedly. "I just want things with Nora to be good again," she said.

Kate nodded but didn't say anything in response. It was the same thing Nora had said about Lucy. But in Lucy's case, Kate wasn't convinced that she wanted things to work out at all. There was something disturbing about Lucy Reilly, and Kate didn't like it. The girl was strange—edgy and unpredictable. Kate found herself wondering what exactly Alice and Lucy talked about.

Lucy looked out the window again and sighed. "There's a storm coming," she said. "A big storm."

"Why do you say that?" asked Kate, looking out at a clear sky.

Lucy laughed. "Just because Mary is bound by the talisman doesn't mean she still doesn't have some powers," she said. "Trust me, she wants a battle. She wants revenge. She's been waiting a long time. And it's coming."

"Then we have to stop her," Kate said firmly, trying to drive the point home. She wanted Lucy to really believe that they were on her side.

Lucy nodded. "Yes," she said. "We do."

Before they could continue the conversation, Jackson entered the room. "Good morning!" he called out cheerfully. "Are you all ready for another day of introspection and self-discovery?"

The class gathered around him in the center of the room and sat in a circle. Kate couldn't help but notice that Lucy once again sat as far away from her as possible. *She still doesn't trust me*, she thought miserably. But she'd done everything that she could. Now it was all up to Lucy.

"For the past two days we've worked with secrets," he said. "Like divers, we've gone beneath the surface of our lives and the lives of our pathmates, returning with things to share. Now we're going to go one step farther. Tomorrow is the Winter Solstice, the longest night of the year. How prepared are you to enter the darkness of that night?"

Jackson looked around the circle, examining the faces of the people sitting there. "The journey into the darkness of the Winter Solstice is a lonely one," he said. "It is long and cold and hard. Are you ready to step into the frozen hours of the solstice?"

Nobody answered him. But although she was silent, Kate was thinking about Jackson's questions. Was she ready to take a journey into the darkness?

She'd always been afraid of the dark, of the unknown. Even as a little girl she'd always slept with a night-light beside her bed. Waking at night and seeing it burning, she'd been comforted, knowing that the darkness of her bedroom wasn't complete, that she always had the light to guide her if she needed it.

But the darkness of the Winter Solstice was complete. It was black and cold and empty. Yes, there was light at the end of it, but that light came only after a long night of nothingness. Was she ready to face it?

"This morning we're going to do a meditation to prepare ourselves for tomorrow's solstice," Jackson told them all. "Tomorrow night—the longest night—all of the paths will join for an all-night ritual and celebration as we greet the returning light. But today we will be taking a short journey into the darkness to see what awaits us there."

He stood and walked to the windows. He pulled down the shades, covering the view and blocking out the bright sunlight. Then he went to the light switches. With a flick, he plunged the room into darkness. Kate sat in the shadowy gloom, her eyes adjusting to the blackness.

"We're going to do a meditation now," Jackson told them, his voice floating out of the darkness. "Close your eyes and listen to my voice."

Kate dutifully shut her eyes, although she didn't

see how that would make it any darker than it already was. Still, shutting her eyes put her in a different mood, one that was appropriate for meditating. It calmed her and helped her to center and focus her thoughts. She breathed deeply, as she had learned to do in her weekly Wicca study class.

"I want you to imagine yourself in a small cabin," Jackson said. "It can look any way you like. It is your home. Picture it now."

Kate imagined herself inside a small stone house. It was a simple house, with one big room. A fire burned in the fireplace, and she pictured herself sitting at a wooden table. It was a cozy image, and it made her feel relaxed and at home.

"It is winter," continued Jackson. "Outside your cabin, the wind is blowing the snow around. You can hear it howling in the chimney, trying to put out the fire on the hearth."

Kate listened to the wind in her mind. Just as Jackson described, she heard it whistling at the windows and sweeping around the house in a frenzied dance. She looked out the windows and saw the snow lifted up and scattered around like feathers escaping from a pillow being shaken by a giant invisible dog.

"All of a sudden you hear a knock at your front door," said Jackson. "You go to it and open it to see who might be out on a night like this—this longest, coldest night of winter."

Kate saw herself rise and go to the big wooden

door of her cabin. She pulled on the handle, opening it a crack. Cold air swept in, bringing with it some snow as she peered out into the dark. What was she supposed to see? she wondered.

"No one is there," said Jackson, answering that question. "All you see is snow and night. But you heard someone knock. Someone *was* there. Now, looking out through the blowing snow, you see a light moving away from you. Someone is carrying a lantern. That is who knocked on your door."

In her meditation, Kate did indeed see a light bobbing in the blackness. It was some way away from her, and whoever was carrying it was moving very quickly through the snow. She wondered who it could be and where the person was going.

"Will you follow the lantern?" Jackson asked. "Will you see where the one carrying it leads you? Decide now. Will you put on your cloak and go out into the darkness, or will you stay inside and wonder what might have been? The choice is yours."

Kate stood in the doorway of her cabin. Behind her, the warmth of the fire beckoned, calling to her to shut the door and keep the cold and the darkness outside, where it belonged. She knew that all she had to do was push the door closed and she would once again be surrounded by a cocoon of light and security.

But another part of her wanted to step out into the snow, to make her way through the wind and the cold and the dark to see where the lantern bearer was going. There was something waiting out there, something mysterious and possibly even dangerous. If she remained in her cabin, she would never know what it was. Then again, if she ventured out into the darkness she might end up lost and freezing, with nothing to guide her back.

"Come on." The voice whispered in her ear, jerking her out of her meditation and back to the real world. She opened her eyes and saw someone crouching next to her.

"I said come on," the voice whispered again, and Kate realized that it belonged to Lucy.

"Where are we going?" Kate asked, trying to be as quiet as she could be.

"To get the talisman," Lucy answered.

Kate nearly jumped to her feet with excitement. Lucy was going to show her where the talisman was! She'd believed Kate's story. *You mean your lies*, she reminded herself. She hadn't told Lucy the truth, that was for sure. But did it matter? After all, Lucy was the one doing the wrong thing. They were just trying to stop her.

Kate stood up as quietly as she could and looked around. Everyone else was still engrossed in Jackson's meditation. Jackson himself was seated by the fireplace. *Thank Goddess his eyes are closed, too*, Kate thought as she and Lucy snuck out of the room and into the hallway. Once they were away from the library door, Kate turned to the other girl. "So you *do* know where it is?" she asked.

"Part of me still doesn't want to tell you," Lucy said. "I've been keeping this secret for a long time."

"But you're doing the right thing," said Kate reassuringly. "Once we get that talisman, we can make everything right again."

"I hope so," remarked Lucy. "For the sake of all of us."

Kate followed Lucy as she walked down the hallway toward the lobby. She desperately wanted to ask Lucy where they were going, but she also didn't want to do anything to make Lucy change her mind. She didn't know why the other girl had suddenly decided to lead her to the talisman, but she was glad that she had. Once Kate had it in her possession, then everything would be okay.

Lucy walked into the lobby and stopped. She looked around. Then she turned to Kate. "It's here," she said.

"Here?" Kate repeated, looking around the lobby. "The talisman is hidden in here?"

Lucy nodded. "Where better to hide it than in plain view?" she said, sounding almost proud.

Kate continued to survey the lobby, but she couldn't see anything that might be a hiding place for the talisman. "I don't get it," she said finally.

Lucy pointed, and Kate followed the direction of her gesture. She was indicating the giant Yule tree that stood in the center of the room.

"It's on the tree," said Lucy. "Come on. I'll show you."

She grabbed Kate's hand and dragged her over to the tree. After circling it for a minute, she stopped and pointed to one of the branches. "Right there," she said.

Lucy reached up and removed one of the ornaments from the tree. It was an angel. It was carved out of wood, and its features were painted on. It also had what looked to be real hair sprouting from its head.

"Alice made it," Lucy explained as she cradled the angel ornament in her hand. "The hair is from Mary. That's what gives it its power."

"She made a Christmas tree ornament talisman?" said Kate, not sure she believed what she was hearing.

Lucy nodded. "It was a brilliant idea," she said. "Mary would never think that she would hide such a thing right out in the open. But there it was. And it's been on this tree every year since, along with all the other ornaments."

"I would never have thought to look here," Kate admitted.

"That was the whole idea," said Lucy.

Kate looked at the angel again. Its hands were folded in front of its chest, and it was looking at her with a peaceful expression on its face. She imagined Alice making it, carving the angel's body out of wood and affixing her sister's hair to it. It must have taken a lot of work. *She must have been really determined to stop her*, thought Kate. But now Alice's spell was about to come to an end.

"Can I have it?" Kate asked Lucy.

Lucy looked at her. She was still holding the angel in her hand, and she didn't look as if she wanted to give it up. She kept looking from the angel to Kate, as if there was a battle going on in her mind and she wasn't sure which side was going to win. Then, suddenly, she handed the angel to Kate and let go of it.

"It's yours," she said. "Now it's your responsibility. Make sure you do what's right."

Kate closed her fingers around the angel, feeling the hardness of the wood and the softness of Mary's hair on her skin. She looked at Lucy. "I will," she told her. "You can count on it."

CHAPTER 12

"You got it?" Cooper said in disbelief.

"Don't sound so surprised," Kate retorted. "I'm not *that* bad an actress."

The two of them were standing in the hallway outside the room where the Air path was meeting. Once again, Kate had stood at the door, waiting to catch Cooper's eye. When she had, Cooper had excused herself and gone outside to see what her friend had to tell her. Now she was holding the angel ornament in her hands and examining it closely.

"I just can't believe she gave it to you," Cooper said. "And where is she anyway? Did you knock her out and leave her in a closet or something?"

"I told her that I was going to go hide this in our room," said Kate. "Then I sent her back to our path. I told her that Nora was in your path and that we didn't want her to know that we were on to her and that we had the talisman."

"Good thinking," Cooper said. "You should get

back, too. When we're done for the day we'll get Annie and Sasha and move on to stage two."

"Destroying the talisman," Kate said, nodding.

"You got it," answered Cooper. "Once this thing is gone, Mary's ghost should be able to come through with no problems."

She paused a moment, looking at Kate. "What's wrong?" she asked.

"Nothing," Kate said. "I just feel sorry for Lucy. I don't really think she's a bad person. I think she got mixed up in something she doesn't understand. You know, sort of like when I did that spell to get Scott to fall in love with me?"

"That came out okay, didn't it?" said Cooper.

"More or less," Kate agreed.

"So will this," Cooper told her. "Once we break the spell this thing has over Mary, everything will be fine. I'm sure Lucy will be her old self again, too."

Kate smiled. "I know you're right," she said. "But I still feel bad for her."

"Get back to class," said Cooper. "I'll keep the talisman in my backpack so that Lucy thinks you really did hide it."

"Okay," said Kate. "But don't lose it. That thing is the key to ending this mystery."

Cooper closed her fingers over the wooden angel. "It won't leave my side," she said.

Kate left, and Cooper returned to class. Before rejoining the circle she stopped by her backpack and slipped the angel inside it. Then she resumed her place in the circle. She leaned over to Nora, who was sitting beside her, and whispered, "We got it."

Nora turned her head sharply and stared at Cooper, her eyes wide with excitement. "The talisman?" she said quietly, her voice trembling with excitement.

Cooper nodded, and Nora smiled at her. Her whole face was glowing with joy, and Cooper wanted to give her a big hug. She had some idea of what Nora must be going through. She had felt the same way herself when the ghost of Elizabeth Sanger had come to her asking for help and she hadn't known what to do. It was frustrating and terrifying at the same time. She had felt powerless to do anything useful; it was an awful feeling to know that someone needed her help and she couldn't give it. She imagined Nora must feel the same way. But now everything had changed. Now they had the talisman, and now they could help the ghost of Mary O'Shea find rest.

But that would have to wait. She couldn't just run out of class. Besides, it was only a few more hours. And they had the talisman. What could happen now?

"Where is it?" Nora asked her under her breath.

"It's safe," Cooper said, "in my backpack."

Nora nodded. Cooper turned her attention to Maia. She needed to distract herself so that she didn't obsess over the talisman and what they were going to do with it later on.

"As you all know, tomorrow night is the Winter Solstice," Maia said. "We always celebrate by holding an all-night ritual and party where we meditate, sing, dance, and pretty much have a good time while we wait for the longest night to be over and for the sun to come up. Since we're supposed to be the creative path, we're going to be responsible for leading the chanting. Now, we'll use some of the old favorites, but I thought it would be fun to make up some new ones as well. That's what we're going to do today. I'm going to have you break into four groups and try to come up with some fun new chants."

"This should be interesting," Cooper said to Nora. She was actually looking forward to the exercise. Writing the song earlier in the week had gone well, and she liked coming up with chants. Besides, it would be a great distraction for her and would help keep her mind off the talisman and the ritual she and her friends would be doing with it later.

"Let's go around the circle and count off in fours," Maia said. "That's the easiest way to do this."

They began with the man to Maia's right and went around, each person calling out his or her number. When they were finished, Cooper, a two, stood up. "See you in a bit," she said to Nora, who was a three.

"You're sure Lucy gave you the real talisman, right?" said Nora, looking anxious.

Cooper nodded. "Kate says so," she replied.

"Don't worry. Everything is going to be fine."

Nora smiled. "I know," she said. "It's just that I can't believe you got her to give it to you."

"Hey," Cooper said. "We're not almost-witches for nothing."

Nora laughed. "Have fun with the twos," she said, as she turned and walked over to her group.

Cooper saw the other members of her own group waiting for her in a corner of the room. She went over to them and sat down. After some initial chatter they started working on ideas for a chant, and pretty soon Cooper was engrossed in coming up with something that would rhyme with "winter." It was fifteen minutes later when she looked up, glanced across the room at the group of threes in another part of the room, and saw that Nora wasn't among them.

She must have slipped out for a bathroom break or something, Cooper thought as she wrote out some ideas for lyrics. The pen she was using had started to dry up, and it went out completely, making only scratches on the paper.

"I'll be right back," she told her groupmates. "I have to get another pen."

She walked over to her backpack and picked it up. When she did, it flopped open. Someone had unzipped it. Cooper felt a sense of dread creep over her as she looked inside. The talisman was gone.

She whirled around, searching the room for Nora. But the girl wasn't there. Cooper's mind raced as she tried to piece together what had happened. But there was only one explanation—Nora had taken the talisman and left. But why? And why hadn't she told Cooper what she was doing?

"Look at that snow!"

The sound of someone talking interrupted Cooper's thoughts. She looked to see who had spoken and saw a group of people gathered around the windows. She looked out, curious about what had brought them all running to look outside.

It was snowing. But it wasn't just ordinary snow. It was a blizzard—a whirling tornado of white that had surrounded the hotel while they weren't looking. Gazing out at it, Cooper couldn't believe that the storm had come upon them so quietly, and without warning.

"There must be four inches of snow out there already," said a man standing beside her.

Cooper looked at the sky. It was gray and cloudy, and it made her uneasy. There was something strange about the storm. It was almost as if it was beating at the windows, trying to get in at them. And the timing of it also disturbed her. Why had it come at the same time that Nora had disappeared with the talisman? Cooper didn't want to think that the two things were connected, but the uneasy feeling that had come over her upon finding the talisman gone was growing stronger by the second. She had to find Nora.

She walked quickly out of the room and into

the hallway. She stood there for a moment, trying to decide what to do. Should she go look for Nora by herself, or should she get Kate and Annie to help her? She had no idea where Nora might have gone, and the hotel was huge. She'd be able to cover more ground if her friends helped her.

But was there time? She didn't know how long Nora had been gone. It might be five minutes or it might be twenty. There was no way to tell. And the longer she waited, the more time slipped by. She didn't know what Nora was doing with the talisman, but she had an idea that the girl had taken it somewhere to destroy it on her own. Cooper didn't know why, but she knew that Nora needed her help. If she tried to do anything with the talisman on her own, Cooper didn't know what might happen.

She heard excited shrieks coming from the room behind her, and looked to see what was going on. One of the big windows had blown open, and snow was rushing into the room. Some of her path-mates were attempting to push it closed, struggling against the force of the wind. Cooper watched them, and she made up her mind. She had to find Nora, and she had to find her quickly.

She ran down the hallway to the lobby, hoping against hope that maybe Nora was there waiting for her. But the lobby was empty except for a couple of people sitting on the couches talking and a few other people looking out the windows at the unexpected storm.

Cooper stood beside the Yule tree, staring up at it. The lights twinkled and the ornaments gleamed. She saw her face reflected in the rounded surfaces of the colored glass balls, her features distorted by the curves. She looked at the angels and bears and toy soldiers that hung from the branches. Where would Nora have taken the angel ornament? Where would she go to try to destroy it?

The tower room. The answer came to Cooper in a flash. Of course that's where she would go. It's where she talked to Mary's ghost. What better place would there be?

She raced down the long corridor to the stairs, then dashed up them as quickly as she could. Her breath came hard and her legs began to ache as she ran, and when she finally reached the door at the end of the fourth-floor hallway she was out of breath. She paused at the door for a minute, letting her tired lungs recover, and then reached for the doorknob.

It was locked. She pulled on it as hard as she could, turning it first one way and then the other. But it wouldn't budge. Cooper gave a final tug and then stood there, staring at the unrelenting knob. Was it locked from the inside or the outside? Was Nora in there, or had she never come there at all? There was no way to tell.

She thought about banging on the door and calling Nora's name, but she didn't want Nora to know that she was on to her. If she really was attempting to do the ritual by herself, Cooper didn't want to frighten her. But she also couldn't allow her to do something potentially dangerous without help. If Nora was up there, Cooper had to get to her.

But she might not be in there at all, Cooper thought, arguing with herself. *You might be wasting your time*. She stared hard at the locked door, willing it to open. She even tried the knob again, hoping that maybe something had happened. But it hadn't. She had to choose—find a way in or give up.

The only way to get through the door was to unlock it. Cooper tried to remember how they had gotten in before. Nora had had a key. Where had she gotten it? *From the front desk*, Cooper thought. *The keys are behind the desk*.

She turned and ran back down to the lobby, her feet thundering on the stairs. She knew she must look insane, running like a mad creature, but she didn't care. There was no time to waste. She glanced out the windows as she passed them and saw that the blizzard had intensified. She knew that somehow the snowstorm was connected to whatever Nora was doing with the talisman, and that worried her.

When she reached the front desk she found the same girl working there whom she'd spoken to the day before. Once again the young woman flashed her a smile. "Some storm we're having, isn't it?"

"Yeah," Cooper said. "Look, I need to get into my room and one of my roommates has the key. I can't find her, so I was wondering if you could lend me the spare one. I'll bring it right back."

"Sure," the girl said. "What's your room number?"

Cooper put her hand to her head, pretending to be thinking. "Oh, what is it?" she said, feigning forgetfulness. "I always recognize it by the painting outside the door. I never really looked at the number."

"What floor are you on?" the girl tried.

"The fourth," Cooper said, holding her breath.

The girl reached beneath the counter and pulled up a ring of keys. "Here are the fourth-floor keys," she said. "Just take the whole bunch. But you have to promise to bring them *right* back. If Mr. or Mrs. Reilly knew I gave these out they'd have a fit."

"Thank you so much," said Cooper. "I really appreciate it. I'll bring these back as soon as I unlock the door."

She smiled at the girl and then ran as quickly as she could back down the hall. *I really need to start jogging,* she told herself irrelevantly as she tried to ignore the stabbing pain in her side. *I am* way *out of shape.*

She ran up the stairs, taking them two at a time, and sprinted to the door at the end of the hall. She looked at the ring of keys, trying to figure out which one would unlock the door. They were all numbered, and she fumbled through them looking for one that was different from the regular room keys. She finally found one, at the very end, but she didn't know for sure that it would work on the door to the tower room. After all, Nora had told them that nobody ever went up there. It was possible that the key was kept apart from the regular room keys to prevent anyone from unlocking the door.

With trembling hands she put the key into the lock and pushed. For a moment it seemed not to fit. Then it slipped into place. Cooper turned it and felt the rods of the lock sliding back. She pulled the knob and the door swung open, revealing the staircase.

Leaving the keys in the lock, Cooper stepped inside. The light was off, and she was tempted to turn it on, but she thought better of it. Instead, she moved up the stairs as quietly as she could. As she reached the top she saw some kind of light flickering faintly.

"Nora?" she called out softly. "Is that you?"

There was no answer, but Cooper could hear what sounded like someone whispering. She couldn't make out the words, but the voice sounded familiar.

"Nora?" she called again.

She came to the top of the steps and stepped into the room. Nora was there. She was kneeling in the center of a circle of flickering candles. She didn't look up as Cooper walked closer.

"Nora?" Cooper said.

Still Nora didn't look at her or show any sign of knowing that she was there. She continued to kneel, looking down at something in her hands. Cooper knelt beside her, just outside the circle of candles.

"What are you doing?" she asked. She looked down at Nora's hands. They were cupped in her lap, and inside them lay the angel talisman. It had been broken in half, snapped cleanly as if cut by a sharp knife. The two pieces had fallen away from one another, the angel's face cleaved down the center.

"It's over," said Nora suddenly, startling Cooper. She looked up at Cooper. Her eyes were shining, and she was smiling. "After all these years, it's over."

"What did you do?" Cooper asked.

Nora laughed. "I broke her spell," she said. She looked down at the talisman in her hands. "She wasn't so strong after all. I knew I was more powerful."

"Why didn't you wait for me?" asked Cooper. "We were supposed to do the ritual tonight with the others."

"I didn't need any help," Nora said. "I just needed you to find the talisman for me."

Cooper looked at the other girl. Something wasn't right. There was something different about her—the way she spoke, the way she was behaving. It wasn't the same Nora.

A gust of wind rattled the windows in the room. Nora looked up. "Listen to that," she said dreamily. "Isn't it beautiful?" She looked over at Cooper. "I always was good at calling up storms," she said.

"Are you sure you're okay, Nora?" Cooper asked. "What exactly did you do with the talisman?"

Nora cocked her head, a smile spreading across her face. "I'm fine," she said. "But I'm not Nora. I'm Mary. And I have you to thank for helping me open the door."

CHAPTER 13

Annie twitched a little as Ivy laid the first plaster strip over her forehead. It was warm, and a little bead of water ran down her cheek. Ivy wiped it away quickly, then her fingers smoothed the strip over Annie's skin.

She was dead. That's what she kept telling herself. Her eyes were closed, her hands were at her sides, and she was trying not to breathe too deeply. Ivy was preparing her for her journey to the world of the dead.

She had been anxious about dying all night. It was a peculiar feeling, knowing that in the morning someone would be readying her for burial. Even though it was just a ritual, something about it felt very real. She almost wished that she'd been one of the first ones to die, rather than being in the second group. The ones who'd gone first hadn't had much time to think about it. They were alive one minute and dead the next.

But she *had* had time to think about it, and she'd

done a lot of thinking. No, she wasn't really dying. But what if she were? What if she really could know when the time of her death was coming? What would she do on her last day? What would be the last thing she ate? What would be the last thing she said, and who would she say it to?

All of these things had gone through her mind in the past twenty-four hours, and she still didn't have definite answers. There were so many things she wanted to do, so many people she loved, so many things left to say. There was no way she could pick just one of any of them. She needed more time.

Ivy placed a strip across Annie's mouth, her fingers applying pressure as she conformed the strip to the shape of Annie's lips. For a moment Annie panicked. How would she breathe? What if she needed to say something? But then she felt Ivy's hand stroking her hair, and she relaxed. Was this how Ivy had felt yesterday while Annie was making her death mask? Annie was glad that she had thought to reassure Ivy from time to time, and she was even more glad that Ivy was doing it for her now. It made her feel not quite so alone.

As Ivy continued to build the mask over Annie's face, Annie found herself sinking into a kind of meditative state. Her thoughts faded away and she found herself feeling safe and loved. It was an odd feeling, because she felt like she should be more apprehensive about what came next. But she didn't. She just felt calm. As each new bandage covered her face and the light reaching her eyes grew dimmer and dimmer, she let go of her worries and concentrated on the way Ivy was lovingly caring for her.

After what seemed like hours, Ivy smoothed the last plaster strip into place. She ran her hands over Annie's face, lightly touching her nose and eyes and mouth and then stroking her hair. She then moved behind Annie so that Annie's head was nestled in her lap and continued to rub Annie's temples while she sang to her quietly.

"Hush little baby, don't say a word," she sang in a low voice. "Mama's gonna buy you a mockingbird."

Annie listened to the words of the familiar lullaby. At first it seemed like a strange thing for Ivy to be singing. But the more she thought about it, the more Annie realized that what Ivy had just done for her was very much like what someone caring for a baby would do. She had tended to her needs, preparing her for what lay ahead. And given the age difference between them, it really was almost as if Ivy had been caring for someone who could easily have been her daughter.

They sat like that for some time, with Ivy singing one lullaby after another and Annie letting the woman's voice fill her head while she readied herself for the next step. Then Annie heard Ginny call for them to stand up, and she felt Ivy's hands helping her to rise. She stood unsteadily, the loss of her sight making it hard to get her bearings. But every time she stumbled there was Ivy's hand, holding her up.

Ivy led her to the doorway and out onto the lawn. Annie felt the change in air temperature. It was much colder outside. And there was no sun today. She could tell because no warmth touched her bare skin to lessen the bite of the wind, which was blowing steadily. She even felt a few snowflakes touch her hands and neck as they entered the labyrinth and began walking the circular route to the land of the dead.

As they walked, Annie could tell that the path, which had been clear yesterday, was covered in a thin layer of snow. She wondered when it had begun and how much was falling now. But she quickly brushed that thought aside and imagined herself walking the long, spiraling path to the underworld. She let Ivy guide her as she moved forward, sightless, her feet crunching on the snow.

When they reached the center they stood and waited as the others joined them. The wind was blowing harder now, and Annie was really cold. The snow brushed her neck, and she was glad that Ivy was holding her hand and keeping it warm.

"Attendants, leave your dead and return to the land of the living!" Annie heard Ginny calling, her voice faint in the wind.

Ivy let go of Annie's hand. "Safe journey," she whispered in Annie's ear. "I'll be waiting for you."

Then Annie was alone. Suddenly she was freezing. Without Ivy there she felt vulnerable and afraid. The wind picked up, blowing her hair around, and the snow seemed to bite into her skin where it touched her. She imagined herself stranded in a blizzard, not able to see where she was going or what lay ahead of her.

"Return to the land of the living!" called Ginny. "Hurry! Time is short."

Annie stood in the cold, listening to the feet of the attendants as they ran back to the safety and warmth of the hotel. She wanted to follow them, to escape the bitter embrace of the wind and snow. But she knew it was not time yet. She had to wait for Ginny's call.

There was a long silence during which all Annie heard was the wind in her ears. Then came Ginny's voice. "Dead," she cried, "turn your backs on the living. Turn away from them and face the land that is now yours."

Annie turned slowly and faced away from Ginny's voice. She knew that Ivy would be staring at her back, mourning her passing. But what was she facing? What was ahead of her? What awaited her in the land of the dead? Was she ready to find out?

"It is time to remove your masks," called Ginny. "Take them off now."

Annie reached up and felt for the edge of her mask. She slipped her fingers beneath it and gently pried it off. At first it resisted, but with a little effort she felt the hardened plaster separate from the film of petroleum jelly with a soft, sucking sound. Then the mask was in her hands and she was blinking in the gray, fuzzy light.

She looked up at the sky and saw angry clouds and swirls of snow. She couldn't believe how hard it was snowing. In only a short time the storm had doubled its strength, and it seemed to be getting stronger by the minute. The people in the land of the dead had dustings of snow on their clothing and in their hair, and all of them seemed uncomfortably cold.

"Leave your masks and return to us!" Ginny commanded them. "Come now!"

Annie wasted no time in putting her mask in the snow and turning to find the path back. But it had snowed so much that the beautiful circles of the maze had become mere outlines. It was almost as if someone had tried to obscure the path, to keep those who had entered the land of the dead there. Annie sensed the others hesitating as they tried to decide how to leave. Part of her wanted to just run straight across the lines of the labyrinth and back to the land of the living. After all, what difference did it make? But another part of her knew that finding the path was important.

Finally she saw it, a faint outline of a once-clear track. The level of the snow was lower there, but not by much. The falling snow had almost completely filled it in, and the tumbling flakes seemed determined to erase all evidence of the path.

Annie stepped forward, putting her foot on the path. She moved quickly, following the traces of the circles as she traveled toward Ginny and the others.

Her pathmates followed along behind her, stepping into her footprints. Together they journeyed around and around the maze, the circles becoming wider and wider as they reached the outer rings. Then they were walking down the final stretch and into the arms of their waiting friends.

"Get inside," Ivy said as she took Annie's hand and pulled her forward. "It's terrible out here."

They all ran inside as quickly as possible. When the last person was inside, Ginny shut the door and secured it. Shaking the snow from her clothes, she looked at everyone and smiled. "Well, we've never had quite such a dramatic setting for that ritual before," she said. "I think you all made it back from the land of the dead just in time."

As if responding to her, the wind rattled the windows of the room. Annie looked out at the snow and saw nothing but white. *Imagine if we really had been lost in that*, she thought, shivering at the thought.

"What about the masks?" asked a woman standing beside Ginny. "They'll be covered by the snow."

"You don't need those masks now," Ginny told her. "Those are the faces of death. What's important now is the face you created for your new life."

Annie had forgotten about that part of the ritual. She turned to look at the masks they'd made on the first day. As had happened the day before, the masks had been arranged on a table that had been set for a party. Seeing them there, looking so cheerful and full of life, made her happy. She was excited about putting on her face of sunflowers and dancing with the others.

"Annie!"

Annie looked up to see Cooper standing in the doorway. She had a look of fear on her face, and she appeared to be out of breath, as if she had been running hard.

"What's wrong?" Annie asked, going over to her friend.

"It's Nora," answered Cooper. "She destroyed the talisman."

Annie looked puzzled. "What do you mean?" she said. "How did she even get the talisman?"

"Kate got it," Cooper told her. "From Lucy. We were going to do a ritual tonight to destroy it, but Nora stole it from my backpack and did it before I could stop her."

Annie still didn't understand. "But we *wanted* to destroy it," she said. "I know she shouldn't have done it without us, but why do you look so upset?"

Cooper looked at her friend, her eyes dark. "Nora lied to us," she said. "She was using us to help her free Mary's ghost, all right, but she didn't tell us the whole story."

"What do you mean?" Annie asked anxiously. "Is she okay?"

Cooper shook her head. "I don't know," she said. "Mary has taken over her body, and from what I saw, she isn't the friendly ghost Nora wanted us to believe she was."

Annie groaned. "Now what do we do?" she asked.

"We have to get Kate," replied Cooper. "And Lucy," she added. "I think maybe we should have been listening to her all along."

"Annie, are you going to join the party?"

Annie turned and saw Ivy smiling at her. Behind them, the rest of the class was dancing a spiral dance, the newly masked participants laughing and having a good time. Annie badly wanted to join them, to celebrate her successful journey to the land of the dead and back.

"I have to go do something first," she said to Ivy. "But save me a place. I'll try to be back soon."

She turned and followed Cooper, who walked down the hall. As they went to get Kate and Lucy, Cooper told Annie a little more about what had occurred in the tower room.

"I didn't know what was happening at first," Cooper said. "I thought Nora was just fooling around. But you should have seen her face, Annie. It was a totally different person in there."

"What did you do?" Annie asked.

"I got out of there," answered Cooper. "I really felt like whoever Nora had become, she wanted me dead. Her eyes were so cold, so dead. It was like looking into blackness."

"And you think it was Mary?"

Cooper nodded. "She said that's who she was."

"But I don't understand," Annie said. "Nora seemed to really trust her."

"I have a feeling we don't know the real story behind all of this," Cooper said. "Someone has been lying—either Nora or Lucy. We have to find out which of them it was."

They reached Kate's classroom and looked inside. The class was seated in a circle. Jackson was standing in the center, doing something with his hands as he talked.

"What are we going to do?" asked Annie. "We can't just barge in there and drag them out."

"We don't really have a choice," Cooper answered. "We've got to find out what's going on and figure out what to do about Nora, or whoever she is now."

Suddenly the lights in the hallway flickered. They went out for a moment, came back on, and then flickered out again. This time they didn't come back on.

"Now what?" Cooper said in exasperation.

"It's the storm," Annie said. "It knocked out the power."

"Great," replied Cooper. "Just what we need."

"Maybe it is," said Annie. "Look."

The doors to the room were opening, and several of the Water path participants came out to see what was going on. Annie and Cooper took the opportunity to slip inside. They found Kate and

Lucy and took them aside.

"We have a problem," Cooper said. "Nora took the talisman."

"What?" Lucy exclaimed. "How did she get it?" She turned to Kate. "I thought you said you hid it in your room."

"Well, not exactly," Kate said, sounding sheepish. "I hid it, but not in the room. I gave it to Cooper to hold on to."

"It was in my backpack," Cooper said. "Nora took it and ran off before I knew what she'd done."

"Where is it now?" asked Lucy. "We have *got* to get that talisman back or I can't even tell you what kind of trouble there will be."

"That's the thing," Annie said when no one spoke. "Something already *has* happened."

"No," Lucy said, sounding scared.

Cooper nodded. "She broke it," she said. "I found her in the tower room."

Lucy let out a sound like a moan and a cry combined. "No," she said. "No. Tell me it's not true." She put her hands to her face for a moment, then turned to Cooper. "Do you know what this means?" she said angrily. "Do you have *any* idea what you've done?"

"Actually, no," Cooper said. "I was hoping you could tell us. Nora said something about not being Nora anymore. She said she was Mary now."

Lucy was nodding, her hands over her mouth. She seemed to be about ready to burst into tears. "She is Mary now," she said. "Or at least Mary is using her body. That's what she's wanted ever since Nora started talking to her. She wanted a way back here."

"But Nora said that's what *Alice* was trying to get you to do," Kate said.

Lucy sighed. "She lied," she said. "She lied to you. I thought you said you believed me. I thought you were helping me keep the talisman away from her."

Kate, Annie, and Cooper all looked at one another. "We just told you that so you would give us the talisman," Kate said finally. "I'm really sorry, Lucy. Nora convinced us that you were the one we had to be afraid of. We thought we were doing the right thing."

"No," Lucy said. "You were definitely *not* doing the right thing. In fact, you couldn't have done anything more not right if you'd tried. I don't know what we're going to do now. She's out. She's back."

"You mean Mary?" asked Annie.

"Yes, Mary," Lucy said. "She's back, and she's more powerful than ever. This storm is proof of it. I told you that yesterday."

"What is she going to try to do now?" Cooper asked.

"For starters, she's going to try to kill me," answered Lucy. "Then she's going to try to complete the spell she left unfinished when Alice killed her, the spell that will make her more powerful than anyone can imagine."

"And how do we stop her?" Kate asked.

Lucy looked at her sadly. "I have no idea," she said.

CHAPTER 14

As the girls entered the lobby the lights flickered back on, although they weren't as bright as they usually were.

"The generator," Lucy said. "Mr. Greaves must have gotten the generator running."

"That's one good thing," Cooper replied. "But it doesn't solve our big problem."

"Lucy, have you seen your sister?"

The girls turned to see Mrs. Reilly standing behind them. "I've been looking all over for her," she said.

Lucy shot a glance at the others. "No," she said. "I haven't seen her."

"I think she was going to go work on a project for our path," Cooper said. "We're supposed to be writing chants for tomorrow, and she wanted some peace and quiet."

"Okay," Mrs. Reilly said. "Well, if you see her, tell her I'm looking for her."

"Is the power going to be on full strength

soon?" Annie asked Mrs. Reilly. "I, um, need to use my hair dryer tonight."

"We don't know yet," answered Lucy's mother. "Mr. Greaves is trying to reach the nearest village to see what's going on there. If a line is down between here and there, it could be out for a while. But don't worry, our generator will keep us going as long as we need it to."

She left the girls and went to speak to one of the hotel workers. A moment after her departure, Sasha appeared. "There you are," she said. "What's up with the power?"

"That's the least of our worries," Annie informed her.

Sasha looked at their faces. "I take it this isn't good?" she asked.

"It's *so* not good," Kate answered.

"Lucy, I think we owe you an apology," Cooper said. "And you'll get it. But first maybe you should tell us exactly what's going on here. Let's go to our room. I have a feeling this isn't something we want to be talking about here."

They went upstairs to the girls' room. The lights there were rather dim, so they lit some candles that had been set out on the dressers to provide a little more light. Once that was done, they sat on the beds and waited for Lucy to tell them her story.

"I don't even really know where to start," she said, looking at the four of them. "I don't know what Nora told you, so I don't know what you know and what you don't know."

"Just start at the beginning," suggested Annie. "Nora told us that she found a diary."

Lucy nodded. "That's right," she said. "She found Mary O'Shea's diary. When she first showed it to me we were both really excited. We'd heard about the O'Shea girls a little bit, but no one was ever able to tell us much about them. Only Mr. Greaves really knew anything, and he didn't seem to want to talk about it. I think the fact that they were twins and Nora and I are twins freaked him out a little."

"What was in the diary?" asked Cooper. "Nora said it was just the usual stuff."

Lucy laughed. "It was hardly the usual stuff," she told them. "It was all about these powers that Mary and Alice had. Nora and I were really excited about that because she and I have always been able to do some stuff that we knew was a little bit different, and we'd never read about anyone else who could."

"Like what?" Sasha inquired.

"Well, we've always been able to tell what the other is thinking, for one thing," answered Lucy. "We assumed that was just a twin thing, though, so we never really thought about it. But we could do other things, too, like make people do what we wanted them to. Nora was always more into that than I was, but we could both do it."

"How?" Cooper asked her.

"A lot of different ways," Lucy answered. "Dolls,

charms, runes—we tried all kinds of things. We didn't understand what any of it was when we were little. We were just fooling around. And when we got old enough to understand it better, we stopped doing it. At least I did."

"But Nora didn't?" said Kate.

Lucy shook her head. "She liked that she could control people," she said. "I kept telling her that it wasn't right, that you aren't supposed to use your powers to make people do things against their will. But she thought it was funny. And she never did anything really hurtful. Not until she found the diary anyway."

"Why?" asked Annie. "What was in the diary?"

Lucy stood up and began pacing. "The summer before Mary and Alice died, a gardener came to work at the hotel."

"Right," Cooper said. "Nora mentioned that. She said Alice was in love with him but that he loved Mary."

"As usual, she gave you the reverse of the real story," Lucy informed her. "At least partly. Alice *was* in love with him. His name was Porter Wills, and he was in love with Alice, too. He used to bring her roses from the garden, and she would make him picnic lunches that they would eat together by the pond."

"Let me guess," Sasha said. "Evil Mary had a thing for Porter, too."

"Yes," Lucy said. "She did. She hated that he was

in love with Alice and not with her. She did everything she could to break them apart. Several times she even impersonated Alice. They looked exactly alike, so much so that even their parents sometimes had a hard time telling them apart. But Porter always knew when Mary was trying to betray her sister, and he never fell for her. That made her madder than anything."

"Mr. Greaves said that a young gardener died here that summer," Cooper said. "I don't suppose that gardener was Porter by any chance?"

"He drowned in the pond," Lucy replied. "Everybody thought it was an accident. Even Alice did at first. She was heartbroken, and she couldn't believe her sister would do something so horrible. Mary even pretended to be sad for her. But four months later Alice stumbled across Mary's diary, and that's when she learned the truth. Mary had done a spell to cause Porter's death."

"And that's when she made the talisman to bind her and keep her from using her powers?" suggested Annie.

"Right," Lucy confirmed. "She didn't want to hurt her sister, but she knew she had to be stopped. Alice thought the talisman would keep Mary under control long enough for her to figure out what to do next."

"Only it didn't," Sasha said. The others looked at her. "Hey," she said, "like anybody couldn't see that one coming?"

"No, it didn't stop her," said Lucy. "She found out what Alice had done and she was furious. She made all kinds of threats. She said she was going to make Alice pay for trying to stop her. And she did. She put spells on her that made her very sick. The doctors couldn't figure out what was wrong, and Alice couldn't tell them the truth. They would never have believed her. She got sicker and sicker. Then, on the night of the Winter Solstice, Alice knew she had to do something. It wasn't just the Solstice, it was the night of their sixteenth birthdays. Alice had read in Mary's diary that she was planning a ritual for that night—a ritual that would make her incredibly powerful."

"What kind of ritual?" asked Kate, not sure she wanted to hear the answer.

"Mary thought that if she killed her sister, she would gain all of her powers," Lucy said.

"But that's not witchcraft!" protested Annie. "No witch would hurt any living thing as part of a spell or a ritual!"

"I know that," said Lucy. "But you have to understand that Mary was pretty much crazy at that point. She didn't know anything about real witchcraft. Her only experiences with magic were the ones that involved manipulating people. She didn't know about the Rede, or about the Law of Three. She thought that she could get what she wanted whatever it took. She'd already caused Porter's death. I think she just convinced herself that it was all a game."

"So Alice went to the tower room on the evening of the Solstice?" Cooper said. "And she tried to stop Mary?"

"You know the rest," Lucy said. "Alice could barely get out of bed. Getting into the tower room took all of her remaining strength. When she got there she pleaded with Mary not to do anything. She tried to reason with her. At first Mary pretended to listen. She helped Alice to the walkway, telling her she needed some fresh air. When they were out there, she pushed Alice over the edge."

"Only Alice hung on," Annie said sadly.

"Alice wasn't stupid," Lucy answered, sounding proud. "She knew what Mary was going to do, and she let her take her to that walkway."

"Why?" asked Sasha angrily. "If she knew Mary was going to try to kill her, why did she do it?"

Lucy smiled sadly. "Because she knew it had to end," she said. "She knew Mary was too far gone. The evil magic had gotten inside of her, and it was growing blacker and blacker every day."

"So why didn't she just push *her* off?" Sasha said indignantly.

"You don't know what it's like being a twin," Lucy said quietly. "You don't know what it's like to look at someone who looks exactly like you, who likes the same things you do, and who half of the time is thinking exactly the same thoughts that you are. When Alice looked at Mary, she saw the other half of herself. She couldn't stand to see her sister being eaten alive by the evil that was inside her, and she knew that if her sister died she would be incredibly lonely, even after everything that had happened between them."

Lucy paused and looked away. It was obvious that she was thinking about her own sister, but no one questioned her. When she looked back at them, her eyes were wet. "In the end she did the only thing she could," Lucy said. "She pretended to be weaker than she was. And when Mary pushed her from the walkway, Alice grabbed her and held on with everything she had left. She pulled Mary off with her, and she held her in her arms as they fell."

Again there was silence as everyone took in what Lucy was saying. Then Cooper asked, "Nora told me that you talk to Alice's ghost. I assume that's true?"

Lucy nodded in confirmation. "After we read the diary, Nora suggested that we try to contact the sisters," said Lucy. "I didn't want to do it at all, but Nora can be really stubborn when she wants to be. Finally, I gave in just to shut her up. So we did a séance in the tower room. That was when Mary appeared. She told us that the diary was actually Alice's, and that it was all lies. She asked us to help her find the talisman so that she could come back to this world to finish something she'd left undone. But when I asked her what that was, she wouldn't really say. That made me suspicious, but Nora believed every word of it."

"But you had the talisman," said Kate. "How did you get it?"

"Alice told me where it was," Lucy answered. "A few weeks after the séance, I went down to the pond one night. I'd been having this recurring dream about being in a boat on the pond and hearing someone call to me. The person was standing on the end of the dock, and I would row toward it. But I kept waking up before I reached it and saw who it was. It was making me nuts, so I decided to actually go there and see if anything happened. That's when Alice first appeared to me."

"She was the person on the dock?" asked Annie.

"She was standing on the end of it, looking into the water," Lucy said. "She was looking for Porter. When I saw her I was convinced I was still dreaming. But then she spoke to me. I've been talking to her on and off ever since."

"When was the last time you spoke to her?" Cooper asked.

"A few weeks ago," said Lucy. "I've been trying to contact her but she doesn't appear. I think as the Solstice nears and Mary's powers grow it's harder for Alice to come through. I think Mary still has some power over her. The last time we spoke she told me where the talisman was and what it looked like. She made it into a Christmas tree ornament because she knew that Mary would never think of that. Only then I went and handed it right over to her."

"No, you didn't," said Kate. "*We* did. You handed it over to us."

"I think this is where the apology comes in," said Cooper. "Lucy, we can't tell you how sorry we are. Nora really had us fooled. She said that you were acting weird because you were under Alice's control and . . . well—" Cooper paused.

"You *were* acting weird," Sasha finished.

"That's not the most tactful way to put it," Kate said. "But yeah. You were acting a little sketchy."

Lucy nodded. "I know," she said. "And *I* apologize for that. It's just been really stressful dealing with this. Nora and I have always been best friends. But ever since Mary started telling Nora that she would help her gain all of these powers, she hasn't been the same."

"Let's talk about that," said Cooper. "What exactly has Mary promised Nora?"

"There was a page missing from the diary," Lucy said. "Apparently it contained the instructions for the ritual that Mary was doing when Alice interrupted her. I know Nora has looked all over the hotel for it and hasn't found it. I looked, too, but I didn't find it either."

"Maybe it's gone," Cooper suggested. "After all, paper doesn't really hold up all that well over that long a period of time."

Lucy shook her head. "It's here," she said. "Mary swears it is. She wanted Nora to help her get through to this world so that she could get it. In exchange, she promised to give Nora some incredible powers."

"But now Mary *is* back here," Annie pointed out. "If what Cooper saw was real, anyway."

"Oh, it was real," said Cooper. "Trust me, I wouldn't run from something unless it was *really* scary."

"Then if Mary is back, that means she's probably looking for the page from the diary right now," Kate said. "She might already have it."

"But why would she want the instructions for the ritual?" asked Sasha. "If it involved killing her sister—or whatever she was going to do—wouldn't she need Alice here for it to work?"

"Not if she had a substitute," said Cooper after a moment's thought.

"What do you mean by that?" Lucy asked, her voice trembling.

"You said it yourself," said Cooper. "The similarities between you and Nora and Mary and Alice are pretty incredible. You were born on the same day. You have similar powers. You're related. Maybe Mary thinks she can substitute you for Alice."

Lucy shut her eyes.

"You told me you were afraid that Nora was going to try to kill you," Kate said. "In path. Remember?"

Lucy nodded. "I was just trying to get you to listen to me," she said. "I never thought she would really do something like that."

"It's not her," Annie reminded Lucy. "It's Mary. She's using Nora to get what she wants. You have to remember that."

"We still have to stop her," Cooper said. "Which means we have to find her. Do you have any idea at all where she might be?" she asked Lucy.

"None," Lucy said. "Although with this storm as fierce as it is, I'm pretty sure she must be inside somewhere. That at least narrows it down."

"We're going to have to find her," said Cooper. "To do that we're going to need all the help we can get. Do you think you can contact Alice?"

"Definitely not from inside the hotel," Lucy said. "I've never been able to do that, and now with Mary back I'm sure it would be impossible."

"Then we have to go to the pond," Cooper said.

"The pond?" Annie, Kate, and Sasha said in unison.

"Hello?" Sasha said. "Let me make the introductions. Cooper, blizzard. Blizzard, Cooper."

"I know it's snowing," said Cooper. "But we need to contact Alice if we can. And I think that if the five of us work together we have a good chance of doing it. So get your coats. We're going on a field trip."

CHAPTER 15

"If everyone will quiet down for a minute, this will be a lot easier."

The murmur of voices ceased and everybody looked at Bryan Reilly, who was standing in front of the Yule tree, the lights of which had been turned off to save power. The room was filled with people getting ready to go to dinner, but now they waited to see what the hotel owner had to say.

"As many of you may have noticed, we're having quite a storm," Mr. Reilly said, earning laughter from the assembled group.

"You may also have noticed our little lighting problem earlier this afternoon," Bryan continued. This time no one laughed.

"The power lines to the hotel have been downed by the storm," said Bryan. "We're in contact with the local power company by radio, and they're aware of the problem. However, the storm is so severe that they can't send equipment through right now, which means we'll have to wait for this to blow through before we can get back to full speed."

"How bad is the storm?" someone called out.

"That's the strange thing," answered Bryan. "No one really knows. This was completely unpredicted, and as far as anyone can tell, the blizzard is concentrated only in our area."

"Big shock," said Cooper to Annie, Kate, Sasha, and Lucy. The five of them were standing in the back of the room, attempting to remain out of sight while they listened to Lucy's father speak. They were holding their coats in their arms, as they had been on their way out of the hotel when they'd stumbled into the impromptu meeting.

"You still think this is Mary's doing?" Annie asked.

Lucy nodded emphatically. "I know it is," she said. "It's the same kind of storm she raised on the night she and Alice died. It's like her energy just causes it to happen."

"The good news is that our generator is running," Mr. Reilly continued. "We don't expect there to be any further problems, but we do ask that all of you do what you can to conserve power. That means no running hair dryers and things of that nature, and we'd appreciate it if you could use the lights in your rooms as little as possible. Other than that, things should be nice and cozy. Dinner is waiting for you, and then I know Bilbo and the others have planned some special events for this evening.

So go enjoy yourselves."

People started to talk among themselves again as the meeting broke up. Then Bryan Reilly returned. "One more thing," he called out in a loud voice. "This is very important. Please don't anybody leave the hotel while the storm is in progress. I can tell you that it's wild out there, folks. We don't want anyone going outside and getting lost in this stuff. So please, stay inside."

Once again people began talking, some of them heading off to the dining room and some of them choosing to sit in the lobby with their friends. The five girls stood there for a moment, looking at one another.

"You heard the man," Kate said. "No going outside. You know what that means."

"Right," said Cooper. "We have to make sure no one sees us."

Kate grinned. "I knew you'd know," she said. "Let's go."

They walked quickly down the hallway, with Lucy leading them. She turned down a smaller hallway off the main one, which took them to a door.

"This leads to the gardens," she said. "We can walk through there and then down to the pond. But it's going to be tricky. The path is downhill, and it's sure to be slippery."

"Everybody stick close together," Cooper said. "If you get separated, stand still and wait for the rest of us to find you. Nobody wander off. Got it?"

Everyone nodded.

"Then let's roll," said Cooper. "We have a ghost to find."

They zipped up their jackets, pulling the hoods over their heads, and slipped on their gloves. Then Lucy pushed open the door and they stepped into the blizzard.

It hit them with staggering force, the wind pushing them back and the snow blowing in their faces. A roaring filled their ears, making it impossible to hear anything. And now that they were away from the lights of the hotel, they couldn't see more than a few inches in front of them.

Lucy took the lead, motioning for the others to follow her. They lined up behind her, sticking close to one another as she pushed against the wind and made her way slowly through the frozen garden. The bushes and the remains of the summer flowers were now only rounded mounds of snow, and it felt like they were walking through some kind of alien landscape. They themselves looked like spacemen, their coats now covered in snow, as they laboriously lifted their feet and put them down again, taking slow, small steps.

They made it through the garden and onto the path leading to the pond. As Lucy had warned them, it was rough going. The path wound down steeply, following the ridge of the hill that the hotel sat on. It was narrow, and with the snow and wind making things even more treacherous, they had to be extremely careful. More than once one of the girls slipped and fell, only to be pulled up by the others.

Finally they reached the bottom. Before them lay the pond, its surface covered with ice and snow. To one side was a dock with a small boathouse at the end. It was toward this structure that Lucy led them, bending into the wind as it seemed to try harder than ever to force them to turn back. But eventually they reached the door of the boathouse, and Lucy, with a thrust of her shoulder, pushed it open. She stumbled inside, the others following after her.

"I've never been so cold in my life," said Sasha, shaking the snow from her jacket and stamping her feet to remove the ice from her boots.

"That storm is *not* natural," agreed Kate, pulling her hood back and breathing into her hands to warm them.

Cooper looked around the boathouse. "Does that fireplace work?" she asked Lucy.

Lucy nodded. "It should," she said.

"Good," Cooper replied, going over to the hearth. She picked up some old newspaper that was sitting in a pile nearby, then turned to Lucy. "Matches?" she asked.

Lucy walked to a small cupboard hanging on the wall and opened it. She pulled out some matches and brought them to Cooper. "There's a little fire-wood there," she said, nodding toward a small stack of logs against the wall. "We had a cookout down here during the summer. That was left over."

Cooper bunched up some newspapers and laid them in the fireplace. Then she took a few of the smaller logs and placed them on top of the balled-up paper. Taking a match from the box, she struck it and held the flame to the paper. It crackled and burned, and moments later the logs began to smoke, then caught fire. As soon as they were lit, the others gathered around, their hands held out to the tiny flames.

"Who knew you were such a Girl Scout," Kate said to Cooper as the logs burned more brightly.

"No Scouts for me," said Cooper. "I just like to play with matches."

The fire began crackling in earnest, and soon the small room was filled with light and warmth. Now that they could see, the girls looked around. The boathouse was filled with all kinds of things that could be used on the pond—a rowboat, life vests, and fishing equipment. A battered couch sat against one wall, and various odds and ends were scattered around the floor.

"How are we going to contact Alice?" asked Kate as they sat in front of the fire.

"You said that you've only ever been able to get her to materialize on the dock, right?" Cooper asked Lucy.

"Right," Lucy answered, nodding.

"Then that's where we should try," Cooper said.

"You mean go back out into that?" Sasha said.

She looked longingly at the fire. "Why can't we just try it in here?"

"Because we need it to work, and we need it to work *now*," Kate said. "If Lucy has always seen Alice's ghost on the dock, that's where we're most likely to get her to show up."

"Kate's right," said Annie. "Cooper initially had the strongest response from Elizabeth Sanger when she went back to the house where she was killed. Our best bet is to try to reach Alice where Lucy has always reached her."

Sasha sighed. "Okay," she said, zipping up her coat again. "But if I get chapped lips because of this I am going to be *really* pissed."

"It's going to be hard to talk when we get out there," Cooper said as they prepared to leave the boathouse. "So here's what we're going to do. We need to create a safe space for Alice to appear. We'll hold hands in a circle. Then each of us should imagine ourselves filled with light."

"Which will be so easy standing in a snowstorm," Annie quipped.

"Once we have our circle established, Lucy, you should call to Alice," Cooper continued. "You know her best, and she'll trust you. Invite her into the circle."

"And if she doesn't come?" Lucy asked.

"We'll worry about that when it happens," Cooper said.

Once more they opened a door and stepped

into the teeth of winter. This time their walk was a short one, but it was made even more dangerous by the fact that they were walking on a narrow dock. On either side of them were the frozen waters of the pond. In places the wind swept back the snow, revealing the black ice, and it gleamed dully.

The girls walked to the end of the dock and formed a circle. Facing one another, they held hands, squeezing one another's fingers tightly. As the storm raged around them they stood silently, each one imagining herself filling with bright light that spilled out and joined with the light of the others to form a ring of shining whiteness. They kept their eyes open, watching one another and trying to ignore the cold that tried to bite through their coats and the wind that tried to pull their hands apart.

"Now!" Cooper yelled above the din of the storm. "Lucy, call Alice now!"

Lucy looked at the others, then called out, "Alice! Please, come to us. We need your help. Please, if you can hear me, I need to talk to you. Mary has come through. We need your help to stop her."

She stopped speaking and waited, looking at the others as they too waited to see whether or not Alice would appear to them. The snow continued to fall hard and fast, and the dock trembled beneath the force of the wind. But nothing happened.

"Alice!" Lucy cried out again. "Please! Appear to us!"

"There!" Annie said suddenly. She dropped Kate's and Sasha's hands and pointed.

At the end of the dock they could see something moving in the snow. At first it just seemed like a shadow. But as it drew closer they saw that it was a figure. It walked toward them slowly, the face still obscured by the snow and the darkness.

"Alice?" Lucy called out hopefully. "Alice? Is it you?"

The figure was hooded. It stopped several feet away from them and its hands reached up to pull back the hood. "No," said a voice. "It's not Alice."

The girls were horrified to see Nora standing on the dock in front of them. She stared at them with an expression of cold rage, her features twisted into a sneer.

"Nora," Lucy said.

"I prefer Mary," Nora said in a voice not her own. "I think it suits me better, don't you?"

"I still like Nora," said Lucy nervously.

Nora laughed. "Do you?" she said, taking a step closer and causing Lucy to stumble back a little. "I suppose you would. Not that it really matters."

"What do you want?" Lucy asked. "Why are you here?"

Nora laughed. "You know why I'm here," she said. "I have unfinished business in this place, and I need you to help me complete it."

"I don't know where the diary page is," stammered Lucy. "I don't."

"I know you don't," Nora replied. "And neither does Alice, so calling her isn't going to help you. Not that it matters. Soon you'll be joining her anyway."

Lucy looked over at Sasha, Kate, Cooper, and Annie, who were standing at the side of the dock.

"Don't look to your friends for help," Nora said, advancing slowly. "They can't do anything either. You know that."

"Oh, yeah?" said Sasha. "How about this?"

She ran forward and slammed into Nora as hard as she could. For a moment it looked as if Nora would fall down from the blow. But the next thing that happened was that Sasha went flying through the air backward. Her friends watched in horror as she arced through the snowy air and over the edge of a dock, landing with a thud on the ice, where she lay, not moving.

"Sasha!" Annie called.

Sasha groaned.

"We have to get her off the ice," Annie said.

She started to lower herself from the dock onto the frozen pond, but as her foot touched the surface there was a creaking sound. A line appeared on the ice, extending out from Annie's foot toward Sasha.

"Get back!" Cooper yelled, grabbing Annie's arm.

Annie scrambled back onto the dock, watching in horror as the ice continued to crack. The dark line raced toward Sasha like a thread spinning out uncontrollably. Sasha was trying to sit up, pushing herself with her hands, but she kept slipping.

"Come on, Sasha," cried Kate. "Move!"

Sasha looked at them as if she couldn't quite hear what they were saying. Then she looked down. The crack had reached her, and now it was spreading out, forming a web of thin lines beneath her. Too late, she realized what was happening. She started to scramble, her feet and hands slipping on the snowy ice. She screamed in terror.

And then the ice shattered. With a horrifying crunching sound, Sasha fell through into the pond. Her friends looked on, helpless, as she sank beneath the ice. Her hands flailed at the water, but she was quickly dragged under.

"We have to get her!" Kate said, jumping from the dock with Cooper and Annie and gingerly approaching the hole Sasha had made.

Nora was still standing there, smiling. "One down," she said. Then she turned to Lucy. "And one more to go."

She stepped toward Lucy, her hand outstretched. Lucy began to babble in fear, holding up her hands to protect herself against whatever was coming. Kate and Annie looked on while Cooper half submerged herself in the freezing water of the hole in the pond, desperately fishing for Sasha. They knew that they could do nothing more for Lucy and concentrated on trying to find some way to save Sasha, who had not reappeared in the hole in the ice.

Suddenly there was a flash of light. Nora

stopped, startled, and shielded her eyes. Then the light dimmed, and another figure was standing on the dock between Nora and Lucy. It was a girl.

"Hello, sister," she said.

"Alice!" Lucy cried out.

Nora laughed. "You came after all," she said. "But I have no need of you. It's the living girl I need."

"You cannot have her," said Alice quietly.

"Can't I?" Nora said tauntingly. "I have already taken one life tonight. What will prevent me from taking another?" She glanced at the pond, where the water visible through the hole in the ice was deadly still.

"Don't be so sure of yourself, sister," answered Alice.

The sound of churning water filled the air, and suddenly Sasha's head broke through the surface. She gasped in great mouthfuls of air, the darkness around her clouding with the force of her frantic breathing. Cooper grabbed her, and Kate and Annie hauled them up.

"What?" cried Nora, clearly enraged. "No, I won't allow this." She glared at Alice.

"Get her into the boathouse," Alice said to Kate, Annie, and Cooper.

Nodding, the three girls lifted Sasha to her feet. She was shaking with cold, but she was able to stumble along with their help as they pushed her through the snowstorm to the boathouse.

"What about Lucy?" Annie cried as they went.

"Alice will take care of her," Cooper said. "We have to get Sasha inside before she freezes."

They reached the door and opened it. Carrying Sasha inside, they brought her to the fireplace and immediately began to remove her wet clothes. Cooper pulled her own jacket off and wrapped her friend in it as soon as she was out of the wet things.

"So cold," Sasha said. "I'm so cold."

"I know," Cooper said, hugging her tightly. "Just sit here by the fire."

"Here," Kate said. "I found this." She brought over a big blanket and put it around Sasha's shivering body. Cooper, Kate, and Annie sat close to their friend, rubbing her and keeping her warm as the fire dried her and she warmed up.

"Can you tell us what happened?" Cooper asked after a few minutes.

"I was sinking," said Sasha. "It was so cold I couldn't feel anything. I knew I was going to drown. Then someone grabbed me and started pulling me back up. That's all I remember. Where's Lucy?" Sasha suddenly asked.

The others looked at one another, their faces grim in the firelight.

"We're not sure," Cooper said. "We left her out there when we carried you in here."

Sasha groaned. "You have to help her," she said.

Before anyone could answer, the door blew open and Lucy came into the boathouse. She shut the door behind her.

"Is she okay?" she asked.

"Yes," answered Annie. "What about you? What happened out there?"

"I don't really know," Lucy said. "It all happened so quickly. Nora came at me and Alice made this bright light appear. Nora turned and ran. Then Alice gave me this." She held up a key.

"What is it for?" asked Annie.

"I don't know," said Lucy. "Alice faded away before she could tell me. I think driving Nora off wore her out."

"We'll have to figure out what that opens once we get Sasha back to the hotel," Cooper said. "We can't stay here much longer."

"I'm worried about my sister, or whoever she is. How much longer can she last out in the blizzard?" asked a worried Lucy, of no one in particular.

"There's no way we can help her from here," said Kate.

"If we get back to the hotel, though . . ."

"I think I can make it," Sasha said. "Are my clothes dry?"

"Not even close," said Kate, feeling the damp things that had been laid out by the fire.

"Here," Annie said. "You can wear my snow pants. I have jeans on underneath anyway."

"And you can wear my sweater," said Kate.

"And I know there's a pair of boots around here somewhere," Lucy said. "They're probably too big, but we can stuff newspapers in them."

Piece by piece they got Sasha dressed as well as they could. She kept Cooper's jacket, and Cooper found another blanket to wrap around herself.

"We're going to have to move fast," Cooper said as they prepared to leave. "None of us can afford to be out in this for long—especially Sasha. Are we ready?"

"Ready," the others said in unison.

Cooper threw open the door and they headed out into the storm. Once again the wind was against them, but they struggled through it and up the path to the gardens. When they reached the top of the hill, however, all that met them was blackness. The lights of the hotel were nowhere to be seen. It was as if the entire building had been swallowed up by the snow.

"Oh no," Lucy said as the five of them huddled together. "The power is out."

CHAPTER 16

The hotel was eerily silent when the girls finally reached the unlatched door they'd come through earlier in the evening and made their way back inside. With no electricity, the only light came from candles that had been lit throughout the hotel. Even these illuminated only portions of the hallways, and they found themselves walking through shadowy corridors as they made their way toward the girls' room.

The lobby was a little livelier, as many of the guests had chosen to congregate there to wait out the storm. A fire had been started in the enormous fireplace, and people were sipping cups of cocoa and hot apple cider while they talked. Someone was playing a guitar, and a group of people were singing. Although normally they would have enjoyed the activities, the girls hurried through, not wanting to answer any possible questions about where they'd been and why they were wearing coats. After handing Kate her coat, Annie split off and grabbed a tray containing mugs of cocoa and brought it upstairs with her.

Back in the room, they shed their cold, wet clothing and pulled on their warmest things. Sasha in particular couldn't seem to get warm until she'd put on long underwear, sweatpants, a T-shirt, a sweatshirt, and two pairs of socks. Even then she sat beneath the covers on the bed, sipping her cocoa with the blankets pulled up to her chin. Cooper once again made a fire, this one in the room's small fireplace, and soon enough they were actually feeling cheerful, if still rattled.

"So, who rescued me in the pond?" Sasha asked after a long period during which the only sounds were the crackling of the fire and the sipping of cocoa.

"I think we have a third ghost. Porter Wills, the gardener who drowned in the pond," said Lucy quietly.

"Yes," said Cooper simply.

"Cool," Sasha said. "That's not something that happens every day."

"You're taking it much better than I did when it happened to me," remarked Annie, thinking about the time Elizabeth Sanger's ghost saved her from a bullet.

"Give me time," Sasha replied. "I'm sure tomorrow I'll be totally freaked out. Right now, part of my brain is still frozen."

"We might not have a tomorrow if this keeps

up," Lucy said dejectedly. "Mary's power seems to be getting stronger."

"We have to figure out what that key is to," said Cooper. "That's the key to all of this—pardon the pun."

Lucy pulled the key from her pocket and handed it to Cooper. Cooper turned it over and over in her hand, examining it from every possible angle.

"It's not a room key, I can tell you that much," Lucy said. "It's too small."

"Maybe it's to a box," suggested Annie. "Maybe Alice hid something in a box that we can use against Mary."

"It's too big for that," Cooper said.

"Too small for a door, too big for a box," said Kate. "This is like Alice trying to find the key to get into the garden in Wonderland. It has to go to *something*."

They sat, thinking, for a long time. Occasionally one or the other of them would throw out a suggestion for what the key might be for, but always there was some reason why it wasn't right. They were getting discouraged and frustrated. They knew that Mary was out there somewhere, working on whatever plan she had to complete her return to the real world, and that made them even more anxious.

"Time is running out," Kate said after no one had made any suggestions for a long time.

Punctuating her remark, somewhere down the hall a clock began to chime the hour. Its deep voice reverberated through the silence of the room.

"That thing has been driving me nuts," Cooper said. "Every time it does that I wake up."

"Just be glad the really big one isn't working," Lucy said.

"Really big one?" repeated Cooper.

Lucy nodded. "The one in the lobby. It was built at the same time as the hotel. Only it hasn't worked in years because the key to open it was—"

She paused and looked at the key that was still in Cooper's hand.

"Lost," she finished.

Cooper held up the key. "Maybe we just found it," she said.

"A key to a clock?" said Annie. "Why would that help us fight Mary?"

"Maybe it won't," Cooper said. "But we're going to find out."

They got up and left the room, practically running down the hall and then down the stairs to the lobby. It was strangely empty when they arrived, as if everyone had gone to their rooms to sleep and left it for them to explore. The fire was burning down in the fireplace, and in the center of the room the shadow of the Yule tree towered over them.

Lucy led them to the wall opposite the reception desk. She pointed to a spot about twelve feet above the floor, where the round face of a clock looked back at them.

"You probably didn't notice it because it wasn't chiming," she said.

"So where does the key go?" asked Cooper, not seeing a door.

"Watch," Lucy replied. "This is kind of cool." She went to the wall and began running her hands over the carved wood paneling that covered it to a height of about four feet. A design of roses and vines ran along the top, and this is what she was touching. After a minute of hesitant fumbling, she found what she was looking for.

"Here it is," she said.

The others moved closer to see what she was talking about. It was difficult to see, so Annie picked up a candle from a nearby table, lit it using a pack of matches someone had left nearby, and held it close to the wall. Then they could see that Lucy's finger was on a keyhole that had been built into one of the roses in the carved design.

"They built the door into the wall," Lucy explained. "But we never had the key so we could never open it."

"Never say never," Cooper told her, taking the key from her pocket. She held it close to the keyhole.

"It looks about right," Sasha said.

Cooper took a deep breath. "Here goes nothing," she said as she slid the key into the hole, where it fit perfectly. She turned it in one direction and nothing happened. The key didn't even move. But then she turned it in the other direction and suddenly a panel in the wall swung outward.

"Mystery solved," Cooper said. "At least part of it, anyway. Who wants to go first?"

"I will," Lucy said.

She opened the door wider and, taking the candle from Annie, stepped through. She was followed by Sasha, Kate, and Annie, with Cooper bringing up the rear. They had to stoop to get through the door, and once inside they found themselves in a narrow, low-ceilinged hallway. Lucy crept along it, holding the candle in front of her.

The hallway ended a few minutes later at another door. When they stopped before it, Kate sighed. "Great, another door and no other key," she said.

"We don't need one," said Lucy, trying the handle of the door and finding that it opened easily. She peered inside. "It's a room," she said.

They stepped into the room. It was small, and there was very little in it. A small wooden table and a chair sat in the middle of the room, and beside it was a stack of old books and papers. Annie went over and began to examine them. She picked up a paper and peered at it in the dim light.

"It's a letter," she said after a moment. "From Porter to Alice."

"My hero!" interjected the bundled-up Sasha.

"Read it," Cooper said.

Annie cleared her throat. "Dear Alice," she read. "I know this will be hard for you to hear, but I feel that I must go away. Things with Mary have become strained, and she has changed. I do not think it is safe for you if I continue to stay here. Please know that I love you with all of my heart, and that one day I will return for you. Until then, keep yourself safe. I do not know what madness has overtaken your sister, but I fear for you both if it remains unchecked. Please, for my sake, take great care. And remember that we will be together again one day, and soon. All my love, Porter."

Annie looked at the paper for a moment longer. "It's dated August 3, 1873."

"He must have written it just before he drowned," said Lucy.

Annie placed the letter back on the desk and began to look at what else was there. She glanced at the books and put them aside, but she looked at the papers carefully. "These are Alice's notes about the spells she did," she said. "It's like her own *Book of Shadows* or something." She looked closely at a piece of browned paper. "A spell for fighting sadness," she read. "It sounds a lot like one of the meditations we do in class."

"So Alice had her own little secret room just like Mary did," said Cooper. "But how is that going to help us?"

"Maybe this will," Annie said. She held up a piece of paper that had been folded into quarters and stuck between the pages of a notebook.

"What is it?" asked Sasha.

"The missing page from Mary's diary," Annie replied.

The other girls went over to see what Annie was looking at. She sat in the chair and spread the paper out on the desk so that they could all look at it at once. It was brittle and brown with age, and the edges were crumbling. On it were drawn several diagrams, and there were lines for a spell scrawled all over it. The girls had just started to read it when a noise startled them.

"I should thank you for doing my work for me," said Nora, stepping into the room. "I had no idea my sister was so clever. On that point I underestimated her. But now it doesn't matter. I have what I need. Give me the paper."

"Or what?" Sasha said.

Nora laughed. "Have you forgotten already what the cold kiss of the pond felt like?" she said. "Perhaps a taste of fire would remind you?"

"Meaning what?" Annie shot back.

A cruel smile spread across Nora's face. "This hotel is old," she said. "It would burn quickly, don't you think?"

"So would this paper," Annie said, holding the edge of the paper close to the candle flame.

"If you burn the paper I will burn the hotel anyway," said Nora coldly. "But if you give it to me I will let you live. Some of you anyway." She looked at her sister, who looked at Annie.

"Don't burn it," she said. "Give it to her."

"What?" said Cooper. "What do you mean, give it to her?"

"I don't want anyone else to get hurt," said Lucy. "Just give it to her."

"But—" Kate began.

"You should listen to her," said Nora.

"Why should we trust you?" snapped Sasha. "Look what you did already."

"Yes," said Nora. "Look what I did already. And that was just the beginning. If you don't give me the paper, you'll see what else I can do."

"Give it to her," said Lucy again. "Please."

Annie took the paper away from the candle flame. She handed it to Lucy. "You give it to her," she said. "I can't."

Lucy walked over to Nora and held out the paper. "Here," she said. "Now leave them alone."

Nora took the paper, folded it, and put it in her pocket. "It's not them I want," she said. "It's you." She grabbed Lucy by the wrist, and Lucy cried out in pain.

"Let her go!" Cooper said, but Nora was already dragging Lucy from the room.

"Don't follow us," Nora warned Cooper. "Stay here until we are gone. Then you may leave. But be warned—any more interference from you and you will all meet the same fate."

Cooper started forward again, but Kate and

Sasha held her back. "Don't," Kate said.

"But we can't just let her take Lucy," Cooper said.

"We'll figure something out," said Kate. "Just don't make things worse right now."

"Worse?" Cooper scoffed. "How could they be worse? Nora has Lucy *and* the spell. We have nothing."

"Actually, we have something," Annie said.

The others turned to look at her.

"What do we have?" asked Cooper doubtfully.

"We have the spell," Annie said, holding up a piece of paper.

"What are you talking about?" said Kate. "You gave Nora the spell."

"I gave her a *copy* of the spell," Annie replied. "Apparently, Alice copied it into her own notebook, too, probably in case Mary found the original. See, here it is."

The others gathered around the table again, looking at the paper. Like the other one, it was covered with diagrams and lines of text, although in a much neater handwriting.

"I noticed it right before Nora appeared," said Annie. "I hid the notebook on my lap so that Nora wouldn't see it."

"Okay, so we have the spell," Sasha said. "But so does Nora. *And* she has Lucy. That still puts her one up on us."

"I know," Annie admitted. "But at least this way

we can figure out exactly what she's going to try to do tomorrow night. Maybe then we can think of a way to stop her from doing it."

"Let's take this back to the room," Cooper said. "We should also bring the rest of the stuff, just in case."

They each gathered up an armload of books and papers, clearing the floor of the mess. Then they left the room, advancing back down the hallway. When they reached the lobby they climbed out and looked around. It was still empty. Cooper shut the door and locked it again, pocketing the key.

The girls went back to their room. There they sat on one bed with the paper in the center as they all read the lines of neat but tiny handwriting. After a few minutes Annie looked up.

"Is this for real?" she asked.

"It looks like it," said Cooper.

"We've never seen anything like this before," Kate remarked. "It looks like Mary is really going to kill Lucy."

"But that's not Wicca," objected Sasha. "No way, no how."

Annie sighed. "No, it isn't witchcraft," she said. "But it *is* something that people used to do in certain cultures. They believed that by killing someone you could gain that person's strengths or powers. Apparently, Mary thought that she could gain Alice's powers in the same way. But Alice killed her instead, so it didn't work. Now Mary has taken over Nora's body and she's using her, and she thinks that if she kills Lucy she'll get *her* powers and be unstoppable."

"Now we know what she's up to," Kate said. "So how do we stop her?"

"That's the part I haven't figured out yet," Annie said. "I have to think about it."

"Don't think too long," said Cooper. "It's almost morning already. Today is Yule, and tonight is when Mary-Nora-Whoever-she-is is going to make her move. We need to figure something out before then."

Annie rubbed her eyes. "I know," she said. "I know."

"Do you think we should ask for some help on this one?" said Kate quietly.

"You mean tell Sophia?" Cooper asked.

Kate nodded. "This isn't like we just did a spell that worked out wrong," Kate said. "This is some-one's life."

Cooper looked at Sasha and Annie. "What do you guys think?" she asked.

"I think that if I were Lucy I would want all the help I could get," Annie said.

"This is all new to me," said Sasha. "I know *I* could use all the help I can get."

Cooper nodded. "I think I'm with you guys on this one. Let's find Sophia."

CHAPTER 17

"You three have gotten into some weird things since I've known you, but this one beats everything," Sophia said. Then she turned to Sasha. "And *you* aren't even in the dedicant class yet. I hate to see what happens to you next year."

"It's not like we asked for it," Cooper said defensively.

"I know," Sophia said gently. "I'm not blaming you for any of this."

They were all standing in Sophia's room. Half an hour before, they had woken her. After much telling and retelling of the story of the past few days, Sophia had been brought up to speed. Now she sat in a chair; she was dressed in her robe. Outside, the blackness of night had given way to the gray of morning, and the room was lit with watery light amplified only slightly by the fire burning in the fireplace.

"Do you really think Nora is going to try to kill Lucy?" asked Kate.

"From what you've told me, it isn't Nora who's doing anything at all," Sophia answered. "It's Mary. For all intents and purposes, Nora isn't involved in this at all."

"Except that she believed what Mary's ghost told her and went along with it all," Cooper said.

"Who was all upset about feeling blamed just a moment ago?" asked Sophia, raising an eyebrow.

"Sorry," said Cooper. "But Nora didn't have to do what she did."

Sophia sighed. "Power is hard to resist," she said. "We don't know what Mary promised her. She just made a mistake."

"But killing Nora?" said Annie.

"If Mary is as unbalanced as Lucy says she is, then I wouldn't disbelieve anything," Sophia answered. She picked up the paper that Annie had given to her and looked at it. "But it looks like she's not so much planning on killing her as she is draining her of her power," she said. "Although if she overdoes it Lucy could definitely end up damaged."

"Should we tell Mr. and Mrs. Reilly?" Annie asked, voicing the question that had been nagging at her ever since Nora had dragged Lucy out of the hidden room.

The others looked at Sophia, who was studying the paper intently. She looked up at them.

"Yes," she said. "We will. But not everything."

"Not everything?" Cooper said. "Which part of everything do we leave out?"

"I'm going to tell them that Lucy and Nora have been influenced by the ghosts in the hotel," Sophia said. "That will be hard enough for them to accept."

"Don't you think they deserve to know how serious things are?" asked Annie.

"I have an idea," Sophia answered. "For it to work, everyone involved has got to be in the right frame of mind. Telling Bryan and Fiona that their daughters are in grave danger won't help things. It will just make them worry, and that will upset the energy of what we need to do."

"What *do* we need to do?" asked Kate.

"A Yule ritual," Sophia told her. "Today is the shortest day and the longest night. It was the birthday of Alice and Mary O'Shea, and it's the birthday of Nora and Lucy Reilly. That's why Mary wants to perform her ritual tonight. Not only is it her birthday, but it's the day when the light and the dark battle for control of the world. She wants the darkness to win out over the light. To fight her, we have to make sure that doesn't happen. We have to fight her with all the light we can summon up."

"Just tell us what to do," Annie replied.

"You're each going to need to use your greatest strengths," said Sophia. "You're going to have to work together and draw on everything you've learned about ritual and magic so far this year. Now, I'm going to have to talk to some of the other leaders here and get their help. We'll all meet and decide how best to approach this. In the meantime,

I'd better go find Bryan and Fiona and tell them the girls are missing. That should be a wonderful way to start the day."

"Do you want us to go with you?" asked Cooper.

"That might be a good idea," Sophia said. "I'm sure they're going to have questions that I can't answer."

Sophia dressed, and the five of them went downstairs. It was very early, and the lobby was still deserted. But a worried-looking Bryan was standing behind the counter when they appeared.

"Have any of you seen Nora or Lucy?" he asked. "We haven't been able to find them all night."

"They were with us," said Kate, and Bryan's face relaxed.

"I hoped they were just hanging out with friends and fell asleep," he said. "It's so unlike them not to check in with us."

"But they're not with us now," said Annie, causing a puzzled expression to return to Bryan's face.

"Where are they, then?" he asked.

"We need to talk to you and Fiona," said Sophia kindly.

Ten minutes later they were all seated in the Reillys' private living quarters, drinking hot tea while Mr. and Mrs. Reilly sat on the couch.

"Sophia, what's going on?" Mrs. Reilly asked. "Where are my girls?"

"Somewhere in the hotel," Sophia said.

"But you don't know where?" asked Mr. Reilly.

Sophia shook her head. "They're hiding," she said vaguely.

"What?" asked Bryan. "Why would they do that?"

Sophia took a sip of tea and held the mug in her hands, as if the warmth of the rising steam helped her think more clearly. "You know how we always joke about the hotel's being haunted?" Sophia asked.

Mr. and Mrs. Reilly nodded. "But those are just stories," Fiona said. "What does that have to do with my daughters?"

"The hotel *is* haunted," Cooper said.

The Reillys looked at her. "What do you mean?" asked Mrs. Reilly.

"Two girls died here many years ago," Annie explained.

"Yes," Bryan said. "The O'Shea girls. They were distantly related to our family."

"Well, they're back," Cooper said. "And Nora and Lucy have been talking to them."

Mrs. Reilly put her hand to her head. "I don't believe this," she said. "Why are you making up such a story? Where are Nora and Lucy? Did they put you up to this?"

"It's not a story!" said Sasha, standing up. "You have to believe us! There *are* ghosts here. Mary tried to kill me by pushing me in the pond, just like she killed Porter Wills. And now she's got Lucy. Well, Nora does, because Mary is using her body and—"

"What Sasha means is that the girls have been influenced by the ghosts of these dead girls," Sophia said as Cooper and Annie pulled Sasha back down on the couch and made her sit quietly. "We think that they feel a connection to them because of sharing a birthday and because of also being twins."

"That still doesn't explain where they *are*," Bryan said.

"They're hiding," Cooper said. "We think they're planning some kind of ritual for this evening—something involving the ghosts of Mary and Alice O'Shea."

"Then we just have to find them," said Mrs. Reilly. "I don't understand why we're sitting here talking about this. They have to be somewhere in the hotel. We'll just search every room."

"Fiona, I know how you must feel," Sophia said. "But I think we need to leave the girls alone for now. They're confused and upset. Trying to find them would only make things worse. Besides, we have another idea."

Mrs. Reilly looked at her husband, who said after a moment, "Sophia has never steered us wrong before."

"Okay," Mrs. Reilly said. "Let's hear it."

"I think we need to go forward with our Yule ritual," Sophia said. "I believe it will draw the girls out of hiding. Then we can do what we need to do to help them."

Mrs. Reilly looked at all of them for a long moment. "Okay," she said finally. "I can't say that I understand any of this—and I think there's more going on here than you're telling me—but I trust you, Sophia, and I trust anyone you call your friend. So I'm going to pretend that everything is fine and leave it in your hands. Besides, I have a lot of hungry guests waiting for breakfast and only three gas stoves to work with. I have enough to worry about today."

"And I have a generator that went kaput for no apparent reason," Mr. Reilly added. "So, like my wife, I, too, will assume that everything is going to be fine, although I'm sure I'll have to remind myself of that every five minutes or so."

Sophia reached over and took their hands in hers. "It *will* be fine," she said. "It will."

They left the Reillys and walked back to the lobby, where they saw Thea, Thatcher, Archer, and some of the others straggling in looking tired.

"Somebody point me to the coffee," Archer said. "If I'm going to last through the longest night I need caffeine in my body."

"Coffee will have to wait," Sophia told her.

Archer blinked. She looked at Thatcher and Thea. "Why do I think this means we're all in trouble?"

"No trouble," Sophia said. "It's more of a . . . project."

Archer groaned. "Even worse," she said. "All right. Let us have it."

Sophia took them to a couch in the corner of the lobby and filled them in on what was happening. As each detail unfolded, Archer's eyes got bigger and bigger. When Sophia was finished she looked at Annie, Sasha, Kate, and Cooper. "Well," she said. "You guys have certainly brought a lot of excitement to our quiet little circle."

"So what exactly do you want us to do?" Thatcher asked Sophia.

"I want a Yule ritual to beat all Yule rituals," Sophia said. "I want singing. I want dancing. I want fires and merrymaking."

"You got it," Thatcher said. "I'll handle the merrymaking and fires. And I'm sure Luna will be glad to help out with the dancing and Maia with the singing. We'll give you a Yule ritual, all right."

"I'll see what kind of decorating I can do," Archer said. "But can I *please* have some coffee first?"

"Yes," Sophia said. "And thank you, all of you. I know we'd all planned on an uneventful Yule celebration, but maybe this is what we needed."

Thea turned to Sasha. "Now let's talk about this falling-in-the-lake thing," she said sternly.

Sasha groaned. "I knew I should have left that part out," she said, looking helplessly at her friends.

Sophia told the girls to go get something to eat while she and Thatcher spoke to the leaders of the four paths and made plans for the evening's activities. Cooper, Annie, Sasha, and Kate went into the dining room, where Fiona Reilly and her staff had managed to pull together breakfast despite having no electricity. The girls piled their plates with eggs, sausages, toast, and other things and sat down at a table to talk.

"Do you think this will work?" Kate asked as she spread strawberry jam on her toast.

"It has to," Annie replied, spooning some hot oatmeal into her mouth.

"I don't know," Cooper said. "I still feel like we should be *doing* something. Maybe Mrs. Reilly was right—maybe we should be searching the hotel. I mean, Nora has to have Lucy *somewhere*, right? Maybe we could find her."

Sasha bit into a sausage link. "You guys are always telling me that you can't force magic, right?" she said thoughtfully. "That you have to let things happen the way they need to happen."

"True," Annie said. "If you try to make magic do what you want it to, it usually backfires."

"Then I think we should wait," said Sasha. "This is all about magic, right? It's about Yule and the struggle between darkness and light. Whatever Mary is planning, it has to happen tonight, when the light and dark are changing places. If we try to stop it before then, maybe we'll throw everything off."

The others stopped eating and looked at her. Then Cooper said, "For someone who hasn't even been in class, you've got a better grip on this than we have."

Sasha laughed. "I think the dunking in the lake woke me up," she said.

"So we wait," said Kate a moment later. "But we have to be part of this somehow."

"I think we're about to find out how," Cooper remarked. "Here comes Sophia."

Sophia arrived at the table and sat down. "Okay," she said. "I have your assignments. Cooper, you're going to work with Maia on music. Kate, you're going to help Jackson organize the ritual. Annie, you're going to help Archer and Ginny with some decorating ideas they have. And Sasha, you're going to help Luna with the dancing."

"So basically we're doing what we've been working on all week?" Cooper said.

Sophia nodded. "You didn't think you chose your paths by accident, did you?" she said. "Now, get going. We have a lot of work to do before tonight."

"You still haven't told us how this is all going to help us find out where Nora has Lucy," Annie said.

"I think if we do this right Nora and Lucy will come to *us*," Sophia answered. "You just worry about doing your parts."

The girls hastily finished their breakfasts and then went to their various classrooms. For the rest of the day they barely had time to even think about Nora and Lucy as they planned, wrote, decorated, and organized. By the time they came together again in the late afternoon, they were tired but excited.

"We came up with some great stuff," Sasha told the others as they prepared in their room for the evening's activities.

"So did we," Cooper said. "It was a little weird because only Maia and I knew what was really going on, but it was like the other people in class somehow sensed that this was really important. We wrote some amazing songs for tonight."

"How did decorating go?" Kate asked Annie.

"Better than I thought it would," Annie told her. "Archer is a genius when it comes to putting things together. Wait until you see the dining room."

The enormous dining room had been off-limits all day as Archer and her crew prepared it for the Yule ritual. Annie, of course, had seen it, but no one else had, and they were all eager to find out what had been done to it.

"What exactly is going to happen?" Cooper asked Kate. "You're the one on the planning committee."

Kate smiled mysteriously. "You'll have to wait to find out," she said. "All I'm going to say is that it's *very* cool."

When they were all dressed they prepared to leave the room and meet everyone else in the lobby, where they had been instructed to gather. Before they left, though, Annie said, "Could we do something before we go down there?"

The others stopped on their way to the door and turned around. "Like what?" Cooper asked.

"I'd like to do a little circling up for a minute," Annie said.

The others walked over to her. Annie took Kate's hand in one of hers and offered the other to Cooper. Cooper and Kate took Sasha's hands. The four of them stood there for a moment in silence. Then Annie spoke.

"I just want to say that you guys are my best friends," she told them. She looked specifically at Kate, knowing they were both thinking about the recent past, and Tyler. "Watching what's happened with Nora and Lucy has made me realize how important family is, even when things aren't going right. You guys are like my sisters, and you're definitely my family. I know things haven't been all that easy lately, but I really love all of you and would do anything for you. That's all I want you to know."

"We love you, too," Cooper said.

"Hey, speak for yourself," Sasha told her. Then she smiled. "I know you three have a special thing going here," she said. "Thanks for letting me be part of it. I never thought when I first saw you at that Ostara ritual last spring that we'd be standing here like this."

"Trust me," Kate said. "Neither did we." She looked at Annie and Cooper. "Annie's right—we are a family. Even when it's tough. And as long as we all stick together, no one is going to get in our way. Not even a ghost with a bad attitude. We took Sherrie down, didn't we? Mary doesn't have a chance."

They all laughed and hugged one another tightly. Then it was out the door and down the stairs. When they reached the lobby they found the doors to the dining room closed. Thatcher and some other people were standing beside some large boxes, out of which they were taking white robes and handing them out to everyone in the lobby. The girls walked up to see what was going on.

"Here you go," Thatcher said, handing them each a robe. "Your outfits for this evening."

"Don't tell me you spent all day making these," Cooper said, pulling the robe over her head.

Thatcher laughed. "No," he answered. "We use these every year. Fiona and Bryan let us store them here."

"Now what are we supposed to do?" Annie asked after they were all outfitted in white.

"Why don't you ask Kate?" Thatcher suggested. "She's the one who planned this."

"Well?" Sasha asked, putting her hands on her hips and turning to Kate.

"We're going to split into two groups," Kate said. "Water and Earth paths down the left-hand corridor and Air and Fire paths down the right-hand one. You'll find out more when you get there."

"More mystery," said Cooper, rolling her eyes.

"Don't worry," Kate replied. "All will be revealed in time."

"Oh, brother," said Annie. She grabbed Kate's hand. "Come on, water girl," she said. "We're going this way."

She started to drag Kate down the left-hand corridor. As they left, Kate turned to Cooper and Sasha. "See you in a little bit," she said, winking.

CHAPTER 18

"Why are we carrying unlit candles?" Annie whispered to Kate as they walked down the hallway. It was difficult to see because all of the candles that had previously lit the corridor had been extinguished.

"I'm not telling you," Kate said. "You'll just have to wait."

Annie groaned and kept walking, following the sound of the drums that were being played somewhere ahead of them. The soft thudding echoed through the corridors as the Earth and Water paths, arranged in two rows of people, made their way slowly toward the lobby. When they reached it, they stopped. Like the hallways, the lobby was in total blackness, and Annie couldn't see anything. She gripped the candle she'd been given tightly and waited to see what would happen.

They stood there in the darkness for some time while the drumming continued. Outside, the snowstorm that had been raging for two days continued, the wind screeching loudly as it buffeted the hotel and rattled the glass in the windows. With no fires burning in the lobby, the air was very cold, and Annie shivered a little. She didn't like being surrounded by the dark and the cold, and she wished something would happen.

Suddenly a spark flared up in the center of the lobby, and Annie saw Bilbo's face illuminated by a candle. Although the flame was small, it made her feel good just to see it. It drove the blackness back just enough, reminding her that there still was light in the world.

"Welcome to the longest night," Bilbo said. "Tonight the world is wrapped in darkness as the reign of winter begins. We are about to enter the hall of the Winter Queen. As you pass by me and into her realm, touch your candles to mine and bring to her the gift of light."

The drummers began playing a different tune, slightly faster than the one that had summoned everyone to the lobby. The columns of people moved forward, and when they reached Bilbo each person touched her or his candle to the one Bilbo was holding. Annie saw that two other lines of people were emerging from the right-hand corridor, so that four people at a time walked toward the doors of the dining room and disappeared inside.

When Kate and Annie came to where Bilbo stood they lit their candles. Cooper and Sasha were there as well, having just come out of their corridor, and together the four of them proceeded into the dining hall.

The tables in the room had been pushed against the back wall so that most of the space was clear. In the center had been erected what looked like a throne. It was draped in white and surrounded by candles, and sitting on it was Sophia. She, too, was dressed in white, and her long dark hair hung loosely about her shoulders. On her head was a crown of holly leaves. She watched, her face impassive, as the people filed in.

"Bring the gift of light to the Queen of Winter," said a voice from the darkness.

The people coming in walked up to the throne and placed their candles on the floor around it. Soon the queen was surrounded by a small circle of light as people presented their candles and then stepped away to stand outside the circle. As Kate, Sasha, Annie, and Cooper came in, they added their own candles to the expanding circle, then went to stand together and wait. They looked at the queen, who seemed to be seated in a pool of fire, as the rest of the participants entered the dining room.

When everyone was inside, the doors to the dining room were shut. The drumming ceased and silence descended as everyone watched the face of the queen. She continued to sit, not moving, for a few minutes more as she stared into the candle flames that surrounded her. Then she looked up.

"I am winter," she said, her voice soft and stern. "I am freezing cold and killing frost. I am blizzard and icicle and howling wind. Tonight I come to claim the world."

The queen stood up and held out her hands. "This place belongs to me," she said. "It is wrapped in darkness and bound by the cold."

She bent down and picked up a candle. "Should I choose to," she said, "I could extinguish all light forever."

She blew out the candle and smiled as a thin stream of smoke floated up from it. Then she looked around at the people watching her. "But perhaps you can change my mind," she said. "Perhaps you can tell me why I should call back the light for you. If you can do that, you may have my blessing."

The queen sat down again. "Let it begin," she said.

The drumming resumed. As they all watched, a group of people walked through the crowd. They were wearing white masks over their faces.

"Those are our death masks!" Annie exclaimed.

The masked people surrounded the queen's throne, facing outward. As the drummers played, the dancers began to circle her, turning their faces first toward her and then toward the assembled group. Then a woman's voice began singing.

"In the bleak midwinter the queen wakes from her sleep," she sang. "She gathers cold about her as she walks in forests deep."

"This is one of mine," said Cooper proudly as

the girls watched the dancers' empty faces. The words of the song mirrored their movements, and they became creatures of the winter worshiping their queen.

"Robes of snow and crown of stars, she rules the frozen land," the woman continued. "All the world slumbers, gone to rest by her command."

The dancers began to spread out, moving through the crowd as the woman continued to sing. The Queen of Winter watched them, a small smile on her face, as they twisted and turned through the group. Sometimes they stopped, their masked faces peering into those of the unmasked before moving on.

"This is creepy and beautiful at the same time," Sasha whispered to the others. "It's like she's putting us all under a spell."

"That was the idea," said Kate.

The Queen of Winter stood up again. "Join the singing," she commanded. "Call to the cold. Call to the darkness."

All around the girls, people took up the song being sung by the lone woman. Their voices filled the room as they welcomed winter in.

"In the house of winter, we gather at her feet," they sang. "On the longest night we wait, the frozen hours to greet."

The song went on, repeating itself several times, as the dancers circled the room. Then one of them took the hand of someone nearby, who took the hand of the next person, and a spiral dance began. Eventually the line of people reached the girls, and the four of them joined the string of hands, holding on to one another as they were swept away in the dance.

The drumming continued as they circled the room. Then the lead dancer moved closer to the queen, forming the first spiral. Around and around they went, the spirals growing tighter and tighter as the white-robed celebrants continued their dance celebrating the Queen of Winter. The song Cooper had written was sung over and over, the many different voices rising up and joining together to create a hypnotic sound.

It seemed that the dance lasted for hours. When the first dancers reached the queen's throne, the spiral began to move out again, with those coming behind intertwining with those making the journey back out. Here and there masked faces continued to appear, and it was as if the winter beings were leading everyone into the darkness of the longest night.

Then the spiral began to open up again as the leader reached the outside of the spiral and drew everyone along the perimeter of the room. The final dancers twirled out of the spiral, and now they all formed one complete circle with the Queen of Winter in the center on her throne.

Only she wasn't alone. As the circle came together and the first and last dancer held hands, they saw that someone was lying on the floor in front of the throne. It was Lucy. She appeared to be asleep. The dancers came to a stop as the drumming abruptly ceased.

"Thank you for your song, and for your dance."

Everyone looked around to see where the voice was coming from. Suddenly Nora stepped from behind the throne and stood beside her sister. Seeing her, Bryan and Fiona Reilly started to step forward, but Nora held up a hand and they froze in place.

"Don't come near," she said, her voice harsh.

"Nora," Mrs. Reilly said.

Nora laughed. "In body, perhaps, but that is all. I am Mary O'Shea, and tonight is *my* night. I have waited many years for this moment, and thanks to all of you, it has come."

Nora looked down at the form of Lucy Reilly. "Tonight I will take what was taken from me by my sister on that Midwinter's Eve so long ago. Tonight I will come to my full power. You have called the blackness in for me. You have raised the energy I need to complete my task. For that I thank you," she said, smiling wickedly.

Nobody moved as Nora bent down next to her sister. It was as if they really were all frozen, held captive by the spell of winter and powerless to do anything to stop her. She lifted her hands over Lucy and began to speak.

"Cold of winter, kiss of death," she intoned. "Blackest hour, frozen breath."

A mist appeared around Lucy and she stirred

slightly, her head moving to the side. Nora ran her hands over Lucy's body and the mist rose, surrounding her hands. Lucy seemed to be having trouble breathing.

"Sister in this frozen hour," Nora cried out in a voice filled with both anger and triumph. "Give to me your magic powers."

The mist around Lucy began to shimmer with a cold silver light. Her face contorted, as if she were in pain. The light moved into Nora's hands, and her face took on an expression of pleasure.

"Yes," she said. "It is working."

Lucy began to writhe on the floor. As more and more of the silver light poured out of her, her body began to fade, as if she were being drained away. Sasha, Annie, Cooper, and Kate watched in terror as she grew fainter and fainter. But still they couldn't move, could do nothing to help their friend.

"Sing."

A faint voice broke the silence. On the throne, Sophia's lips moved slightly as she said again, "Sing. Call back the light."

For a moment there was no response. Then Cooper's voice came through the stillness, faint and strained, as if she had to sing through ice or through the howling wind. "Spark of light, return to us," she said. "Break the spell of winter's cold. As the longest night must end, come and warm the frozen world."

As Cooper sang, her voice grew stronger, as if the cold that surrounded them was melting away.

Soon others began singing as well, joining their voices with hers, and the room filled with the sound of people calling to the light.

Nora looked up, an expression of anger on her face. The silver mist began to recede, resettling around Lucy's body.

"No!" Nora said. "I won't allow this."

She began to speak her chant again, her invocation of dark and cold cutting through the song being sung by the people in the circle.

"Cold of winter, kiss of death," she said.

"Spark of light, return to us," countered the singers.

On the floor, Lucy began to stir. Seeing this, Nora looked around frantically. "Sister, in this frozen hour!" she cried. "Give to me your magic powers."

Suddenly the candles surrounding the Queen of Winter's throne flared up, becoming brighter than ever. Nora threw back her hands to cover her face.

"Sister," said a voice. "It is over."

Alice appeared before the candles, her ghostly form illuminated from behind by their glow so that she seemed filled with fire. Seeing her, Nora stood up.

"You cannot come into this place," she said. "You have no power here."

"They give me power," Alice said, indicating the singers around them. "They give me strength—the strength of the returning light."

Nora looked back at Lucy, who was starting to sit up. She lunged at her, but Alice leaped forward and caught her in an embrace. When she put her arms around Nora, Nora screamed as if she were being burned. Then she collapsed beside Lucy.

A moment later a ghostly form rose from the body of Nora Reilly. Mary O'Shea stood before her sister. She looked down at her insubstantial body and an expression of hatred and defeat came over her.

"It is over," said Alice.

Sophia rose from the throne and stepped down. Facing the two ghosts she said, "The light has returned. The darkness is driven away. Go now, both of you."

The flames of the candles seemed to come together, forming a doorway of flame. Alice turned to it and smiled. Mary backed away.

"No," she said. "I will not be defeated this way."

Alice turned to her sister. Reaching out, she grabbed Mary's wrist. Mary pulled away, but Alice held tightly. Then she stepped forward into the doorway of light. Mary was pulled along with her, crying out in anguish. But as the light touched her, she faded away. A moment later the flames died down again and the candles flickered gently in the stillness.

The singers stopped singing and stared at Sophia. She looked around the room. "Tonight the light has won," she said. "I know many of you do not understand what has just happened, but know that because of you a long darkness has been lifted."

She knelt down beside Nora and Lucy Reilly, both of whom were struggling to sit up. Their parents rushed to them and helped them, holding the girls in their arms.

"What happened?" Lucy asked, looking around.

"I don't really know, honey," said her father, hugging her to him.

"Lucy?" Nora said, rubbing her eyes. "Is Lucy all right?"

"Yes," Mrs. Reilly said, stroking her daughter's hair. "You're both all right."

Cooper, Sasha, Annie, and Kate ran forward to join Sophia and the Reillys. Sophia put her arms around them. "I wasn't sure we were going to pull that off for a minute there," she said. "But you guys did it."

"We *all* did it," Kate said, looking around at the assembled faces, some of whom seemed very perplexed by the incidents of the past hour.

"We'll explain it to them later," Sophia said. "Right now we have some partying to do."

As if confirming her statement, there was a flicker of light and suddenly the electricity came on. A cheer went up from the crowd as people rushed to turn on more lights. Then Cooper looked out one of the windows.

"The storm is over," she said. "The snow has stopped."

Nora and Lucy were standing up now, supported by their parents. The girls went over to them.

"How are you guys?" Annie asked.

"I don't remember much," Nora said. "I feel like I've been asleep for days. What happened?"

"Later," Lucy said, yawning. "Let's just say you owe me *big* time."

"Now what?" Sasha asked Sophia.

"Now we party," answered Sophia, smiling as the drummers began to play once more.

Morning dawned clear and sunny over the hotel. When Kate, Sasha, Cooper, and Annie went downstairs for breakfast they found Nora and Lucy sitting together at a table. After getting their own plates, they joined the sisters.

"Lucy told me what happened," Nora said, sounding embarrassed. "I'm really sorry, you guys. I feel like a total idiot. I should never have believed what Mary told me."

"It's okay," Kate said. "Ghosts can be pretty persuasive."

"And pushy," added Sasha, making them laugh.

"Do you think we'll see either of them again?" Lucy asked.

Cooper shook her head. "I think last night was the big good-bye," she said. "Wherever they are now, they're on their own."

"But look on the bright side," Annie said. "You

still have the murdered honeymooners to talk to if you get bored."

Lucy and Nora looked at one another. "I think we've had enough of ghosts for a *long* time," Nora said.

"You're not giving up on magic altogether though, are you?" Sasha asked.

Again the sisters looked at one another for a moment. "No way," they said in unison.

"Well, here's a little something to get you going," said Cooper. She placed Alice's tattered notebook on the desk. "This baby contains all the spells Alice did. I bet you can learn a lot from it."

"Thanks," Lucy said.

"Consider it a belated birthday present," said Cooper. "We didn't really get to do a real birthday last night, you know."

"I got the best gift I could ever get, though," Nora said, putting her arm around her sister. "I got Lucy back."

"And I got you back," Lucy said. "And none too soon. Let me tell you, Mary was really starting to get on my nerves." She looked at the others. "So, what's on the agenda for today now that the ghost business is cleared up?" she asked.

"Well," Kate said. "We don't leave until tomorrow, and we're pretty much done with our path work. So I was thinking maybe we could build a snow fort and have an all-day snowball fight."

The others glared at her.

"Just kidding," said Kate. "Geesh."

"Give me that spell book," Nora said, taking it and flipping through as the rest of them erupted in laughter. "There's got to be something in there we can use to turn her into a newt."

follow the
circle of three

with book 12:
written in the stars

"The stars are so bright tonight," Annie remarked to Kate and Cooper. "Look at that one just below the moon. It's like someone turned on its high beams or something, especially for New Year's Eve."

"That's not a star," said a woman who had come outside with Archer. "It's a planet. Jupiter, actually."

"Everyone, this is Olivia Sorensen," Archer said as the others looked at the woman. "She's going to be teaching class for the next couple of weeks as we study astrology."

"You're an astrologer?" Kate asked.

"And an astronomer," Olivia answered. "I work for the planetarium. A number of years ago I was asked to write a paper debunking astrology. Unfortunately for the journal that asked me to write the paper, I became a believer instead. Now I do both."

"Olivia is amazing," Archer told the girls. "I

have her do my chart every year, and she always surprises me with how on target she is."

"Well, it *is* a science," Olivia said. "Although I admit that it takes different skills to read an astrological chart correctly. You have to be willing to go beyond the realm of numbers and formulas and see the larger pattern they're a part of."

"Are you a witch?" Sasha asked Olivia.

"Me?" Olivia said, sounding surprised and a little embarrassed. "Sort of. I mean, I'm not *officially* a witch or anything. I don't belong to a coven. But I'm interested in Wicca." She paused for a moment. "I guess you could say that I'm witch lite."

Annie laughed. Olivia glanced at her and smiled shyly, then laughed, too, as if sharing a private joke. The others looked at them in mild amusement. Then Cooper looked at her watch.

"It's almost time for me to be in bed," she said, standing up. "Who wants a ride home?"

"I do," Annie said.

"Kate?" asked Cooper.

"Sure," said Kate. "Let me get my coat."

The girls stood up to say good-bye to their friends. "I guess we'll see you on Tuesday," Annie said to Olivia as they shook hands.

"I'm looking forward to it," Olivia replied.